Tell the World You're a Wildflower

Tell the World You're a Wildflower

stories

JENNIFER HORNE

The University of Alabama Press • Tuscaloosa

Typeface: Garamond Premiere Pro

Cover image: *Red Flower* by Ann Feeney
Design: Michele Myatt Quinn

∞

The paper on which this book is printed meets the minimum require-
ments of American National Standard for Information Sciences—
Permanence of Paper for Printed Library Materials, ANSI Z39.48-1984.

Library of Congress Cataloging-in-Publication Data

Horne, Jennifer.
  [Short stories. Selections]
  Tell the world you're a wildflower : stories / Jennifer Horne.
    pages   cm
  ISBN 978-0-8173-1845-1 (trade cloth : alk. paper) —
ISBN 978-0-8173-8777-8 (e book) 1. Women—Southern
States—Fiction. 2. Southern States—Fiction. I. Title.
PS3608.O76275A6 2014
813'.6—dc23   2013049867

For Dad and Nancy

Contents

Acknowledgments

Grateful acknowledgment is made to the editors of the following journals for first publishing these stories: "Blue," in *Birmingham Arts Journal*; "Business or Pleasure," in *Southern Women's Review*; "1957," in *PMS poemmemoirstory*; "Other People's Dogs," in *Arkansas Literary Forum*; "Sixteen Going On," in *Foliate Oak*; "Why I Live at the Albert Pike Hotel," in *Muscadine Lines*.

Thanks to Don Noble, Mary Horne, Dick and Nancy Horne, Mark Dawson, Gretchen McCullough, and Wendy Reed for their encouragement, and to copyeditor Susan Harris for her fine work, and to editors Dan Waterman and Jon Berry at the UA Press for their steady, capable guidance. Thanks also to the Alabama State Council on the Arts for a Literature Fellowship in 2008.

Tell the World You're a Wildflower

I

Blue

I am sitting in the back seat reading my book, and my mom is in the driver's seat with her head leaned back on the headrest and her eyes closed. We are in the drive-through car wash, basic cycle, for the third time this week, that I know of. Mom says at four dollars a pop it's cheaper than therapy. Dad says Mom needs something to alleviate her stress and that Mom should take up yoga. Mom hates yoga. I heard her telling her best friend Cyd on the phone that if God had meant us to do yoga he wouldn't have invented bourbon. Still, you'd think Dad would notice how clean the car's been lately.

I don't tell Mom because I think it would freak her out, but I have a great idea for a horror movie. It takes place in a car wash. A couple of teenagers go for the deluxe wash so they'll have more time to make out, but when the wash ends there's blood all inside the car windows and the car behind them starts honking for them to move forward, but they've been slashed to pieces by the Car Wash Slasher.

That's why I always make sure the doors are locked while we're in the car wash. A psycho, one who didn't mind getting all wet and soapy, could get in your car and kill you and it would be hard to drive away and no one would even see it happening, especially with the big blue and white ribbons this car wash uses.

Sometimes at night I try to imagine what happens when I go to sleep. Does everything stay in the same place or does it move around and then get back in place before I wake up? Maybe my dog and cat talk to each other. Maybe my hamster opens his cage and goes on adventures.

This is what my teacher Mrs. Huff calls being fanciful. If she called it creative, that would be a positive thing, but fanciful means I make too much up and I'm too much in my own imagination.

As far as I can tell, my family is pretty normal. Our house is like other people's houses, our cars are like other people's cars. Mom and Dad work, like most moms and dads.

Lots of families just have one kid, too. If Mom wouldn't have lost the baby, there'd be two of us, which is also normal. One weird thing about us is that the door to the nursery is always closed now, and sometimes Mom goes in there and cries when she thinks I won't hear her. The nursery is blue, which is a color I am starting not to like. After she lost the baby, she and Dad fought over Dad not having finished putting up the wallpaper, and Dad said it was a moot point now, and Mom just said, "Moot."

Mom and Dad told me about the baby, who would have been my baby brother, although he does not seem real to me any more than praying does. Mom says that in Japan there are shrines for babies who died before they were born and that she wishes we had those here. I don't tell her but I think dead-baby shrines everywhere would be creepy.

When the car wash ends, I like the part where the big frame glides all the way back into place in front of the car, and the sprayers are still dripping a little bit, and the green "THANK YOU" light comes on, and Mom shifts into drive and we go over that little "clunk" place and come out from the dark of the car wash into the light. Mom and I say together, "Out we go," and she always smiles back at me as we turn right onto Cantrell and head toward home.

Truth or Consequences

People might not think I know much on account of being only ten and a girl and living in a small town, but I do. I pay attention, and I learn things. Especially if you are small, people sometimes forget you are there. Then when they remember they will look at each other and point their eyes in your direction and say, "Little pitchers have big ears." But by then you have probably learned a lot that you can think over later and figure out.

I learn stuff from TV, too. I have my own TV in my room and I watch it after school, especially the shows with audiences and a host like for a game show but with people who have made a mess of their lives and want to talk about it. Mothers who fall in love with their daughter's boyfriend. Wives who fall in love with their husband's sister. Teenage girls who get pregnant and don't tell their moms. Men who like to dress up in women's clothes. Old people like grandparents who want to have sex and live together but their kids don't want them to. Sometimes I have to look words up in the dictionary, like "transvestite" and "abortion" and "bisexual" and "penile." I got the dictionary for my tenth birthday.

At six my mom gets home from work and picking up supper, and we sit on the couch and eat in front of the TV in the living room. She likes watching game shows and she is real good at *Jeopardy* and *Wheel of Fortune*. She is smart and knows almost all the answers. "Lotta good it's done me," she says, when I tell her she is smart, but then she hugs me and I know she means about love and marriage and my daddy.

I did not know he was gone for almost a week because my mom said he had to go on a trip and he had to leave too early to say goodbye. When it finally got to be Saturday and he didn't come home she had to tell me that he had left us. She was crying when she told me and I was scared. I only saw her cry once before and that was when my grandma died in a car accident because of a drunk driver. She doesn't cuss, but when that happened she kept saying, "That bastard, that bastard."

I asked her a lot of questions but she didn't know the answers, and that scared me, too. Like why Daddy left, and when was he coming back, and did we do something wrong. All she says is that Daddy needs time to sort some things out, but I don't know what things. She says they married too young and he never sowed his wild oats. At first I thought she said "sewed" but then I looked up "wild oats" and saw I was wrong about that. My dictionary says that wild oats are "misdeeds and indiscretions committed when young." I had to look up a lot of other words just to try to understand that definition. A misdeed is a wrong or illegal deed. An indiscretion is an indiscreet act or remark. Indiscreet is lacking discretion. Discretion is the quality of being discreet. Discreet is marked by, exercising, or showing prudence and wise self-restraint in speech and behavior. Prudence is the state, quality, or manner of being prudent, and prudent is wise in handling practical matters. After all that, I still don't understand what she means, except maybe that Daddy is doing something bad and not being wise.

My favorite game show is an old one called *Truth or Consequences* with Bob Barker. It makes me feel kind of happy to watch it, and I sometimes imagine that I am there and get called out of the audience to answer questions. I come up to the stage and say, "Hi, Mr. Barker, my name is MaryAnne Flowers and I am from the great state of Arkansas." The audience is impressed by my stage presence, and I answer all the questions and win an all-expensive-paid trip to New York City and a lifetime supply of my favorite cereal. Which is Life.

My daddy's name is Darrell Flowers, and he sells supplies to doctors' offices so he travels a lot anyway. But he is always home on weekends, except now he isn't. Mom says that he asks about me when he calls, but he always calls after my bedtime, so I hear the phone ring and then Mom picks up and then she talks in a soft voice, like she is trying to convince him of something. I get a stomach ache lying there in bed, like when Jeannie Maslock punched me in the stomach on the playground. Once I snuck into the kitchen and picked up the phone real quiet and listened.

She said, "I know you need time, but we need you," and he said, "You'll just have to be patient," and then she said, "I have been, but what am I supposed to tell MaryAnne?" and then he sort of got quiet and said, "Tell her I love her and I think about her." Then she said, "What am I supposed to tell her about you being gone?" and he said, "I don't know. Make something up. Just don't tell her I fell in love with a twenty-year-old receptionist," and she said, "No need to rub it in," and I put the phone down. I opened the cabinet door and got a box of Life out and took it to my room and ate it in the dark. I was crying and the salt from my tears got into my mouth with the cereal but I just kept eating until I finally fell asleep.

Sometime in the middle of the night I woke up and found the box on my chest and reached down and put it under my bed. When I turned over and lay still, I could feel a cool breeze on my forehead, a real light breeze, like someone's breath, but cool. It made me feel so good, calm, like everything was going to be all right. It comes back sometimes when I can't sleep, and I think maybe it is my guardian angel. A lot of people on TV think that we all have a guardian angel who looks after us, and I hope I do because I need one. I know that there isn't any Santa Claus or Easter Bunny, but angels live with God, so they are probably real.

Sometimes on *Truth or Consequences* Bob Barker brings out a person from the past, like a contestant's third-grade teacher or scoutmaster or long-lost best friend from camp. If I grew up and my daddy never came back home, and I got on the show, and Bob Barker brought my daddy out and said, "MaryAnne Flowers, here is your father!" I would just say, "Who?" and look like I couldn't care less. I would say, "I think you are on the wrong show. You are supposed to be on the show about fathers who fall in love with receptionists and mess up their lives." Then I think probably Bob Barker would admire me so much that he would ask me to marry him, right then and there, and I would tell him thank you, and that I would consider it but that I also planned to become a pilot. Then he would say, "I respect that, MaryAnne. I'll be here waiting for you," and the audience would applaud without even needing the "Applause" sign to go on, and I would walk up the aisle with everyone standing and clapping as I went by, and I would not look back.

Sixteen Going On

I would like to be named Kate. I would like to have a life list of birds that I began keeping at age six. I would like to be the precocious only child of intellectual but loving parents. I would like to be the middle child in a large ethnic family, boisterous and warm. I would like to live in New York City like Harriet the Spy and drink egg creams. I would like to know what an egg cream is. I would like to know more about the Revolutionary War than the Civil War, aka The War Between the States. I would like to ice-skate outdoors on a frozen pond. I would like to be a surfer girl with hair streaked blond by the California sun and a body hardened by riding waves all day long. I would like to sleep with boys and not care or sleep with boys and care so much I'd drive ninety miles an hour down the highway at midnight to forget them. I would like to have a relative who died in a concentration camp, so I could participate in the suffering of the world. I would like to know the names of trees. I would like to be able to name the constellations. I would like to lie outside on my back at night watching meteor showers without being eaten alive by mosquitoes and no-see-ums. I would like to sail a boat solo around the world and write a book about it. I would like to write my memoirs at age ninety and title them "Confessions of a Free Spirit." I would like to watch every foreign film ever made and know how to pronounce the titles. I would like to speak French fluently, with a slight Lyons accent. I would like to be a black girl with attitude from Chicago. I would like to learn karate so I could take care of myself in a fight. I would like to go to Africa and help AIDS victims. I would like to drive a Jeep across the open desert and sit at the top of a sand dune and watch the sun go down. I would like to have five children, all boys, and take them camping in the Rocky Mountains. I would like to take a train across Canada. I would like to read Dostoevsky, Tolstoy, and Pasternak in Russian. I would like to go far away for college. I would like to study philosophy. I would like to be able to tell a joke, and I would like to speak up when people tell offensive jokes. I would like to study jokes and what makes them funny, or not. I would like to eat blowfish in Japan. I would like to become a Buddhist and visit temples and meditate. I would like to have my portrait painted, nude, by a famous artist. I would like to bathe in the Ganges. I would like to be in a protest march for a noble cause and get arrested and spend the night in jail and wake up stiff and hungry and walk out into the sunshine and go to a diner with my friends and eat a big breakfast and drink lots of coffee and talk and talk and talk.

Mexico

My favorite high school teacher once told us that everyone should collect something. Growing up in Texarkana, Arkansas, a town divided between Arkansas and Texas, I decided to collect the names of places that straddled a border and to try to go to each of them someday: Florala, Alabama; Kanorado, Kansas; Marydel, Maryland; Michiana, Michigan; Cal Nev Ari, Nevada; Texico, New Mexico; Texhoma, Oklahoma, and Texola, Oklahoma, both sharing a border with Texas; Pen Mar, Pennsylvania; Tennga, Tennessee; Virgilana, Virginia. There were also a Texline, Texas, and a Pennline, Pennsylvania, as well as several State Lines and State Line Cities, but to me that just indicates a lack of imagination. Texarkana is by far the largest city of the combo-towns. As far as I can tell there aren't any towns that straddle the United States and Canada, although there is a Sault Ste. Marie in both Michigan and Canada. At California's border, though, there is Calexico. When I first read it, I liked the sound of it: Ca-lex-ico, emphasis on the "lex." It sounded lively, exotic, like a hot pepper.

I did not expect it to be the first town I'd visit, not by a long shot.

When you grow up with a whole other state just across the street, the road is always beckoning. So it was easy to imagine driving southwest toward Dallas, where I had been with my mother several times to shop, and then on across Texas into New Mexico, Arizona, and finally California.

I wasn't actually sure I'd get all the way to California when I started out, but it helps to have a destination. I thought if I could get somewhere very different from home, I could sort it all out, get some perspective on Cody, getting married, the whole shebang.

We had fought, big-time, over our honeymoon destination. He wanted Vegas; I wanted a cruise. He wanted exotic dancers and gambling and a heart-shaped bed, while I dreamed of sunbathing and slow dancing and delicious food. I yelled at him that Vegas was just tacky and he yelled back that I ought to know, a slam on my family's lack of money next to his. I could tell his mother thought that I was "marrying up," despite the fact that his parents were just a step from living in a trailer but had made good with his dad's landscaping business, which had spread out across the state as "Mow for You" Enterprises. Cody's family spends every dollar they make on things people are sure to notice. In contrast, my mom has problems with energy, and so things don't always look too tidy around our house, plus she has an odd sense of lawn decoration, and my dad is an engineer at the plant and doesn't really notice his physical environment, as long as his easy chair remains in the same place, so we're not exactly ready for the *Southern Living* camera crew. But tacky we are not.

It was a long drive, longer than I could've imagined, and as I drove through Texas the green of nicely watered lawns and big sloping trees and even bushes and scrub began to disappear, slowly at first and then more and more quickly until all I could see was variations on brown. I had brought my dad's road atlas, the one his insurance agent gave him, and once I got to Dallas I saw that I could take I-20 through west Texas and then hit I-10 all the way to California. I drove and drove and drove, napped, ate, and peed at rest stops, and listened to CDs over and over again, never allowing a minute to pass without music, knowing that if silence fell I might start to think, and I wasn't ready to think. I just wanted to drive.

I was probably just tired from all that solo driving, but I felt a little let down driving into Calexico, expecting an exotic cross-cultural mecca and finding only what looked like a smallish town with a couple of burger and taco joints and a run-down motel with cabins like the old ones in Hot Springs National Park. Maybe if I'd driven further there would've been more to see, but I was tired and afraid of running out of money and so I just stopped on the edge of town. I went into the glass-walled manager's office and checked in. The middle-aged woman looked at me suspiciously, her leathery arms resting on the high fake-wood counter.

"Just you?"

"Yes, ma'am, just me."

"You ain't got a boyfriend waitin' for you in the car? Price is more for two, you know, plus we charge double if we find out you snuck him in. And we always find out." She looked at me with unblinking eyes, as though she could stare the truth out of me.

"Look, I'm on my own, OK?" I said, getting frustrated. Her tight gray curls and stretch-band Timex wristwatch reminded me of our school nurse, a bitter woman who dispensed tampons and sanitary pads and aspirin and never moved from her sickly-green-painted lair down the hall from the principal's office.

"Looks like a engagement ring to me," she said, moving her eyes to the gold ring with its tiny chip of diamond that Cody had given me.

I looked at it, twisted it off my finger, and slapped it on the counter. "Not anymore," I said. "Take it. I don't want it anymore." Not waiting for her response, I picked up my key, stomped out to the car, and drove to cabin #13. I didn't even worry about it being unlucky.

All the cabins were painted with turquoise trim, including the metal poles that supported the small porches in front of each one. Each porch had two turquoise-painted lawn chairs to match, not the mesh kind or the plastic kind, but those old metal ones with the arms and legs one single piece of bent pipe. My granny has two on her front porch, plus a metal glider, and dealers come by all the time and offer her a hundred dollars for them because they're popular now, but she won't sell them.

Naturally, when I got inside, I had one of those moments when you think what the hell am I doing. The bed was swaybacked like an old horse, the lampshades were stained with age, and, when I went to check out the bathroom, I found a huge almost-dead roach, legs up, in the center of the bathtub.

Then I took a deep breath and reminded myself I was on an adventure, boldly going where no one in my town had ever gone before, pursuing a dream and searching for new frontiers. Who knew what might happen, or who I might meet? I'd heard that a lot of movie stars had houses in southern California, and besides which I'd never been so close to another country. I might even cross over into Mexico, if I could find out whether you needed a passport and where you did it.

I flushed the roach, swished out the tub, and took a nice hot shower. Then I got dressed and went out to find something to eat. At a place called La Chica Bonita I had a frozen margarita and two tacos, plus a lot of chips and guacamole dip. There was really nothing else to do then, so I went back and sat on my little porch and smoked a cigarette, feeling kind of relaxed and easy from the margarita and thinking of how grown up I was to be staying in a motel by myself, planning my own destiny.

Cody and I had stayed in a couple of cheapo motels, but that was different. He rented some porn tapes—which I just really have no taste for, I mean if I am right there completely naked, why should he need more— and bought a couple of six-packs which he had cooled down in the cooler in his trunk, and we did it a couple of times but didn't stay past midnight. After the second time his friend Brady asked me if I had seen any good movies lately, so I knew Cody had been bragging about it, and I wouldn't go anymore. The more I thought about it now, the more I wondered what I'd seen in him in the first place. But then it was all about seeing, and being seen. He was beautiful, blond, and muscled and tan, and I loved the way people looked at me when I was with him. Not that I'm bad looking, but he has something special, something that makes people turn their heads in the store to see if he's really as good as their first glance told them.

Dusk was falling, and I was thinking about heading inside to find something to watch on TV when I suddenly noticed a shadow off to my left, a long, oval, dark spot half on the concrete of the porch, half in the dirt yard, like someone on the side of the cabin, waiting. Without turning my head I watched the shadow. It shifted. My heart pounded and for a minute my eyes went blurry. Was something bad about to happen? I glanced at the other cabins. No one else on their porches. One light on two cabins down. The manager's office had closed at 8:00 P.M. I had to move, but my legs felt frozen in place, so I decided on the count of five I would turn and step just as fast as I could over to the door, which fortunately I had already unlocked. The shadow shifted again, and I caught a glimpse of the worn, pointy toe of a cowboy boot. I leaped inside, slammed the door and locked it, grabbed the knife I had brought with me from my suitcase, and waited.

I heard steps on the porch, shuffling mixed with sand making a shh, shh, shh, shh sound. Then more waiting. My curtains were drawn so I couldn't see out and no one could see in, but I could feel a person outside, and my heart kept pounding until I thought surely I would just have a heart attack and die. I don't know why I didn't call the police, but in my fear I somehow got it in my head that they would speak Spanish, and I couldn't remember anything from seventh grade except my very first dialogue I memorized with Suzanne Compton, my next-door neighbor, who practiced with me at the bus stop until we both had it down perfect:

Está Susana in casa?
Si, está con una amiga.
Donde está, in la sala?
No, in la cocina.

And that did not seem as though it would be very useful.

I pulled the bedspread off the bed and took it and both pillows and my knife into the bathroom and closed and locked the door and made a bed in the bathtub, like my sister and I used to do in tornado season when our parents were both working and the siren went off and we were home by ourselves. We'd take a jar of peanut butter and a spoon and our favorite stuffed animals and a flashlight and wait for the storm to pass. I wished with all my heart she was there with me.

Finally I fell asleep. I woke up and looked at my watch and it was morning and nothing had happened. I realized I had probably overreacted, out of tiredness. And then I started crying, at first I thought from relief and exhaustion, but then from up inside me came the knowledge that something bad had indeed happened and that I had driven a thousand miles not to think about it and had still not outdriven it.

The night before I left, Cody and I had eaten big bowls of ice cream and fresh strawberries with his parents and then gone for a walk on the golf course behind their house. It smelled cool and moist for a warm summer night, and I took off my sandals and felt the soft green clipped grass on my soles. Cody slowed down and took me in his arms. It was the perfect setting for a romantic kiss. When he went to lay me down on the grass I resisted. The grass was damp and I'd get wet and probably get grass stains on my clothes to boot. I didn't want his parents seeing what we'd been doing, as I was still officially a good girl, not like Tammy Taylor, who was known to have done it with practically the whole football team. But he pushed me down anyway.

"Cody," I said, "cut it out!" I could feel the hardness in his jeans.

"Brenda, we're getting married," he said. "It's OK."

"I know, but not here. Not now. Cody, I mean it," I said, and tried to shove him off.

"Fine," he said, still holding me down with one hand. "But this, and this, and this"—he touched each breast and then between my legs—"they're all mine and don't you forget it. Once we get married you can't say no anymore. It's a wife's duty." He was smiling, but in his easy, friendly, southern boy's eyes I caught a glimpse of something mean, something cruel in his desire to have what he wanted, when he wanted it. Then he lifted himself up, leaving me to get up by myself. That was when we fought about the honeymoon, but it wasn't that we were fighting about.

When we got back to the house, I said I was tired and went home early. The rest of my family was on vacation up at Lake Dardanelle, and I had stayed home because I didn't want to be away from Cody for two whole weeks, and he couldn't leave because he had to work for his dad's landscaping business.

I didn't think about anything, just packed my suitcase and took my savings from my underwear drawer and lay in bed until just before dawn, when I locked the house and drove west.

And that was it. That was the bad thing. Not that he had made me have sex when I didn't want to, which he hadn't done, but that he had just as good as told me that he could, once we were married. It made me so sad to think he thought of me that way: as a bunch of parts, titties and pussy, all his. And even sadder to think what it would mean not to marry him, not to be special because of him anymore. What had happened to Brenda the high school volleyball star, Candy Striper, camp counselor? Or Brenda the all-star babysitter? After babysitting MaryAnne Flowers since she was a toddler, I had felt so strong when I was able help her through her parents' split-up. Now I realized I had not thought to make plans beyond "Marry Cody and live happily ever after" and suddenly visiting all the bi-state towns seemed like a pretty poor Plan B.

I hauled everything back to the bed, packed up, and took my stuff out to the car. Just under the left front wheel something glinted at me. I picked it up: a delicate silver ring with a round turquoise in the center and two silver scrolls on the side. It was bent a little from someone, maybe me, driving over it, but the silver was soft and warm from the sun, and I bent it back into shape, carefully feeling as I went how much pressure I could put on the metal without breaking it. Inside the band, the word "MEXICO" was stamped. I slipped it onto the ring finger of my left hand. The blue mirrored the cloudless sky overhead, and the silver seemed like it would hold up for a while, long enough for me to figure out where I was headed next.

"Just Friends" with Jesus

St. Agatha's Cathedral School for Girls
Assembly: November 15, 10:00 A.M.
Subject: Attire
Speaker: Sister Mary Patrick, Principal

Let us pray.

"Hail-Mary-full-of-grace-the-Lord-is-with-thee-Blessed-art-thou-among-women-and-blessed-is-the-fruit-of-thy-womb-Jesus-Holy-Mary-Mother-of-God-pray-for-us-sinners-now-and-at-the-hour-of-our-death-Amen."

Welcome, girls. For those of you just coming in, there are still seats on the bleachers. Sister Mary Thomas, will you be in charge of seating late arrivals and noting their excuses? And Sister Mary Joseph, will you please close that open window by the bleachers? A little bird seems to have flown in through it.

Before I begin with the subject of today's assembly, I have two announcements. First, as you know, our Fall Festival will be held this weekend. All girls are expected to attend and to help out in some way, either in preparation for the festival or staffing booths. Anyone unable to attend due to illness or death in the family should see Sister Mary Eugene.

Secondly, our midterm exam results have been compiled and turned in to my office. I am happy to report that our average GPA has risen this semester over both semesters last year, and I wish to congratulate both our teaching sisters and our students. Now is the time to continue your hard work and dedication and, although of course we all expect to have fun this weekend, it is no time to neglect your studies.

Now girls, that is just a bird. It is one of God's creatures and will not harm us, nor should it distract us. His eye is on the sparrow, but yours should not be. We will deal with it after assembly.

Today's subject is Attire. The Senior Class Committee has, very admirably, made as its goal for the senior class this year to expand and advance students' appreciation of the life of Jesus. Senior Class Committee, will you please stand and be acknowledged? The committee has sponsored weekly New Testament Bible studies on the life of Jesus, established an art contest for portraits of Jesus, and has also sold T-shirts, bracelets, charms, and bumper stickers as part of an "I ♥ Jesus campaign." It is these last items I wish to speak with you about.

Even though these items were chosen with the best intentions, and I have spoken with the Senior Class Committee about this already, we have decided that they perhaps do not represent St. Agatha's or the Christian faith in the best light. Although a number of blessed female saints throughout the centuries have felt themselves to be in a passionate spiritual relationship with our Lord, such language now, in our secular society, is unfortunately open to misinterpretation.

Therefore, you are asked not to wear or display any items stating "Jesus Is Hot," "Me + Jesus," "Savin' It for Jesus," "Going Steady with Jesus," "JC Is My One and Only," "Taken—by Jesus," and "A Date with Jesus Is a Heavenly Experience." Demerits will be issued to students continuing to wear these items, but I hope and trust that will not be necessary.

In place of the "I ♥ Jesus campaign," the Senior Class Committee, in consultation with the faculty administration, is launching a new campaign, "'Just Friends' with Jesus." You will be receiving order forms for new T-shirts, et cetera, which will be available for the spring semester, starting in January. Some suggested slogans are "Jesus Is My Best Friend" and "Jesus's Line Is Never Busy."

Yes, I am aware that the bird has landed on my head. I'm sure he will be—see, he's gone already. As St. Francis said, "Be praised, My Lord, through all your creatures."

Now. As long as we are on the subject of attire, I will just remind you of a few recent infractions that I have seen recently: Peter Pan collars, *not* button-down or pointed collars, are the required shirt collar style; knee socks are to be worn pulled up to just below the knee, not rolled down bobby-sox style; and sparkle makeup is not allowed under any circumstances.

You may now return to your classes in an orderly fashion, senior class first, freshmen last. May the Lord watch over and protect you all and don't forget to keep selling those raffle tickets. Dismissed.

II

Ted and Mary

Last night, as my boyfriend, Joel, and I were fishing Tupperware containers out of the fridge trying to put something together for supper, I found myself thinking "I bet Ted Danson and Mary Steenburgen never do this." I bet they never have an ounce of cooked carrots and some three-day-old spaghetti and some leftover fried chicken and a container of peach yogurt for supper. I imagine they have something healthful, and fresh, and simple yet elegant. Some bok choy, maybe, and some steamed wild rice. Although I do think Ted probably likes a nice juicy steak every once in a while—he looks like a carnivore.

It's not like I came up with Ted and Mary arbitrarily. Since I finished college last year I've been working in a health food store, Joe's Organics, in Little Rock, saving money for grad school. Ted and Mary have a place in Arkansas, and so every once in a while they shop at Joe's, just like normal people. They get a cart and walk up and down the aisles, and the people who shop there are cool so nobody bothers them much. The last time they were in Joe's, Mary was wearing a white cotton camisole and jeans and her hair was a little messy, and Ted was in jeans too but with a long-sleeve shirt like he used to wear on *Cheers*. Joel and I are both too young to have watched *Cheers* when it was first on but we sometimes watch it on reruns late at night when he can't sleep. The television is in the bedroom, which I am pretty sure is some bad feng shui, but Joel insisted on it as a condition of moving in together.

I don't think I'm obsessed with them or anything, not like my mother used to be with Prince Charles and Lady Diana when I was growing up. I haven't seen all their films or TV shows, and I don't buy a lot of magazines with stories about them, and I've only visited their websites a few times, just to check on some things, like how long they've been together, whether they have kids, together or with other people: factual stuff. It's just that, seeing them at the store and all, I wonder about their lives, and I think their lives must be a lot better than mine. Smoother around the edges, cleaner, more fulfilled. When you look at that big, relaxed smile on Mary Steenburgen's face, you think that she knows what happiness is all about and how to get there.

My best friend, Carla, who works next door at the wine store, has what my mother used to call a potty mouth, but I like to think of her as just earthy. When I talk to her on our smoke breaks about Ted and Mary, she says, "Get real, Karen! Don't you think they burp and piss and shit and fart just like the rest of us?" It makes me uncomfortable to hear Carla talk this way about them, as though I am being somehow disloyal, but she also makes me laugh. "You want to break up with Joel, break up with Joel, but don't keep obsessing about Ted and Mary's Perfect Life." That's how she says it, with capital letters you can hear.

Things with Joel are not that great, I admit. Sex lately is more zero-to-sixty-in-thirty-seconds than a nice slow drive through the beautiful countryside ending at a magnificent view. We moved in together last year with plans to get married at Christmas, but it is now July and if I bring it up he just says, "What's the hurry? We're going to be hitched for a lifetime." So mostly I don't bring it up.

Joel says life is imperfect, and we're probably the best either of us is going to do. He does not believe in true love or finding the perfect mate. After seeing my mom go through a boyfriend about every six months, I would hardly call myself a romantic, but I do wonder whether it isn't supposed to be better. Like Ted and Mary. Like people who shop at the local health food store and then go home and cook a nice supper together and talk while they eat instead of watching TV. People who then do the dishes together and sometimes, when their fingers touch as one hands the other a plate to dry, pause and smile at each other because they are happy just to be together, and they know they're lucky.

Noli Me Tangere

So I had this germ thing. More like a contamination thing. I got to where I didn't like to touch anything or for anything to touch me. Which is very tricky, when you start thinking about particles you can't see, things that cling to your skin in the air or that you breathe in without knowing it. Once you get started there's really no end to thinking about it. Like I could get my clothes cleaned at the dry cleaners so they'd be really clean, but then someone would've had to take them out of the cleaning solution and put them down on something and then put them in a bag that had come from who knows where and then the bag would hang next to other people's clothes and other people would be touching the bag, so that when I picked up the bag and took it home I'd have to disinfect my hands before I could touch the clothes, and even then I had the nagging suspicion they weren't really safe. So you can see how my thought processes went when I was in that mode. Mostly now I'm OK. You won't find me using common salt shakers and ketchup bottles, for instance, but I can open doors in public places with my bare hands, I can breathe deeply even in the presence of strong smells, I can hug the people I love and not worry about where they've been or what they have on their clothes. It might not sound like much but it is.

I've tried to think how it started, and I think I know. My first serious boyfriend, Craig, was really into cleanliness. I didn't have much experience at that point, so I didn't know what was normal and what wasn't, but he always insisted we take showers together before and after sex. At first I thought it was pretty romantic, but then sometimes I wouldn't want to and he'd just insist. He said it got him in the mood, but looking back I think he was worried about dirt in its various forms. He threw out food way before its expiration date, and he got his car detailed every week but then he Lysol-ed it afterwards, the entire front seat, because "you know what kind of people work in those places."

When he broke up with me I got really depressed. I started watching a lot of TV, which I don't normally, and I kept seeing all these commercials about germs. Of course the commercials were in the business of selling disinfectants, but they got to me anyway. One showed a woman wiping a raw chicken breast all over her kitchen counters and table, to illustrate how a dirty sponge could spread salmonella. Another showed a guy thinking about all the people who had sat in the airplane seat before him, coughing and vomiting. A third showed kids coming in from school leaving multicolored germ tracks on everything they touched. And then my grocery store started providing free hand sanitizer, which made me think maybe I should be using it. As far as I'm concerned, those commercials should come with a warning label.

Then, though, it was like something had clicked into place inside me, the way pieces of the model airplanes Craig liked to build clicked in perfectly with a satisfying little snap. (Myself, I always liked those balsa-wood planes you bought at the dime store, light but tough two-piece wonders that glided across your back yard, launched by your own hand.) I had a kind of mission, then, of protecting myself from the world. Pretty obvious, right? But I was at a low ebb and it made sense when little else did. Nobody else in my family has had these kind of problems that I know of, unless you count my crazy dancing aunts, so I think it was kind of situational.

I was finishing my master's in early childhood education at Fayetteville, and after Christmas I had to do my student teaching in a local school. It was going to be germy, but I had my hand sanitizer at the ready and I planned to change clothes and shower just as soon as I got home each day. I was placed with first graders—my favorite year—and did a lot of extra tutoring with the kids who weren't quite up to speed with the rest. Most kids now come to first grade already reading some, and it's important to work with the ones who can't so they get a decent start. We'd sit in a corner made cozy with a couch and chairs, a soft rug with squares of different colors, and a couple of giant stuffed animals, a panda and a lion. The kids, two little boys and a girl, would snuggle up to me for reading practice. If they wanted to hold hands, I'd tell them I had to turn the pages, and if they sneezed, I'd tell them to cover their face with the inside of their elbow and get a tissue and use the hand sanitizer.

One day, though, they all had colds. I had to help wipe their noses, and I couldn't get away to wash up, and then I was just so hungry I ate my sandwich while I helped decorate for the school play, and, when I got to the end of the day, I realized I had forgotten, for a little while, to worry. It wasn't until then that I realized how much I actually did worry, how much time it took up, and how it had changed me.

I talked to a counselor at school and I got some medication for a while. Mostly I got back into my life, step by step, and now I can hug my beginning readers when they do well or when they cry or when they run to meet me as I come into the classroom.

Why am I telling you this, this story of how I lost the knack of being at home in my own skin and have had to work to get it back? Why tell a secret that still seems shameful though I am assured it is biochemical, neural, neutral?

So that, if you happen to notice me in the beat between reacting and correcting, between a flickering, mild aversion and its positive revision, you will know that I am on the mend, not the other way round. It's like learning a different route from your usual drive to work, hard at first, highly conscious, but easier each day you go along.

Business or Pleasure

I got into O'Hare late and took a taxi to my hotel. There'd been no food on the airplane, of course, and I was hungry but too tired to find a late-night restaurant. The hotel restaurant had just closed and room service was over, but the desk clerk told me I could get something at the bar. I stuck my carry-on in my room and went back downstairs. Normally I don't go into hotel bars alone—it's just too much trouble trying to make it clear that you're really not interested in male attention. I don't have a boyfriend right now, so I am free to choose, but I feel it's better not to mix business and pleasure. I'm much more comfortable in my room anyway, propped on the bed at ease in my nice pajamas, laptop on my knees, papers spread out around me.

I sat at a table near the bar and ordered a nacho salad and a light beer. While I waited, I browsed the headlines of the paper I'd picked up in the lobby. "Heavy Storms in Southeast Forecast" caught my eye in the weather section. Great. I was likely to have trouble flying back to Little Rock. I was only in town for a day, to take a deposition in a big case I'd been working on for months. This was one of the last pieces we needed to finish our preparations.

As I glanced up, a man sitting at the bar caught my eye and smiled. I smiled back with what I think of as my public-impersonal smile, acknowledging but not encouraging. I don't like to be rude.

"Long day?" he said, in a sympathetic voice.

"Yeah. Late flight, all that."

"Where from?"

"Little Rock."

"No kidding! I've been dying to get down there to see the presidential library and museum. Have you been?"

"Yeah," I said. "It's great. You like Clinton?"

"Always did," he said. "Smart guy. Just couldn't keep it in his pants, you know? Too bad."

I've never really liked that phrase. My face must have betrayed me.

"Sorry," he said. "That was crude. I'm a geologist, been around a crew of guys up in Alaska for three months. I've forgotten my manners."

The server brought my food out at the same time his order arrived.

"You mind?" he said, picking up his plate as though to bring it over, but not pushing.

I hesitated, then said, "Sure."

He was outdoorsy cute, with short brown hair, a tan, and blue eyes that looked like an airline pilot's. I guessed he was maybe thirty, just a couple of years older than me.

"John Bartlett," he said, putting down his plate and beer and holding out his hand.

"Sarah Bailey," I said, shaking his.

"So what do you do?" he asked.

"I'm a lawyer," I said, waiting. I took a bite of my salad, avoiding the sour cream.

"Great," he said. "Great. My ex-wife is married to a lawyer now, actually our divorce lawyer. You'd think that would be unethical or something, but there it is."

"Um," I said.

"But we have a great little girl. Jessica. I hope she can grow up to be independent, confident, have a good job. That's so important for women."

"Yeah," I said, "my parents always encouraged me to do whatever I wanted."

We talked a bit about where we grew up, where we'd been to school, that I was on business for a case and he was spending the night in Chicago after a bad connection made him miss the last flight to Texas, where he had another job.

"Hey," he said. "Change of subject. You are a beautiful and charming woman, and we're both alone here tonight, and I'm sure you never do this kind of thing, but would you consider spending some time with me?"

I looked down at my plate. I was attracted to him, it was late, I was a little lonely, he seemed nice. Just last week my friend Betsy had been kidding me about being absolutely unspontaneous.

I looked back at him. His head was cocked slightly and a questioning smile played across his face. If I said no, it would be OK, would be no big deal, which is why I said yes.

"Come to my room in ten minutes," I said. "543." I stay at this hotel whenever I'm in Chicago, and I didn't want them getting ideas about me.

He smiled. "See you soon."

Riding up in the elevator I felt a kind of nervous energy in my veins, as though I'd had way too much caffeine. Was this OK? Was it? I had "just-in-case" condoms in my overnight bag but couldn't remember how old they were. That was a deal breaker for me, but I somehow didn't think he'd refuse.

I went to the bathroom and brushed my teeth. Fluffed my hair.

The knock on the door came, and I answered it, and he stepped inside and kissed me, then stepped back.

"Just wanted to get that over with," he said, not smiling now. Suddenly it felt serious, not like in the bar.

I stood by the window and he sat down on the bed. "Let me see you undress," he said.

I did, and that sort of broke the tension, and pretty soon we were in bed with the lights out and both of us undressed. With the curtains open, a dim city glow barely lit the room, like a false twilight.

He took his time, kissing and touching me. There'd been no argument about the condom.

I was nervous, but it was exciting. We did a couple of things I hadn't done before. When we actually started to have sex, it was harder than I like, and he didn't ease up when I asked. I started to feel like I was floating outside of myself, looking down, and then it was over.

He lay back, smiling. "Whew. That clears the pipes, huh?"

"Oh, yeah," I said, as though I had done this kind of thing before. Suddenly his whole patter in the bar came back to me, so obviously scripted, rehearsed. Nobody had made me do anything, but I, Sarah Bailey, attorney at law, had let myself be picked up with an obvious line. I thought I knew what I was doing but I didn't know how it would feel afterwards. Even lonelier. Foolish.

He seemed to doze off, and I lay there staring at the ceiling. The floating feeling came back, and the strangest thing happened: I started to lose my sense of being me. As though I was falling down a well and "I" was a circle of light at the top, and I couldn't stop. I was terrified, and I didn't understand what was happening. It seemed to take all my energy to sit up on the edge of the bed and return my self to myself.

My movement woke him up, and I said the first thing I could think of to get him to leave.

"I have to get up really really early," I said. "So . . ."

"Sure," he said. "Use me up and cast me aside. Ha ha."

I sat back up in the bed with the sheets pulled over my breasts.

He got up and pulled on his clothes. "Well, it was fun," he said. "Take it easy. I'll let myself out." And then he was gone.

When the door closed I got up and put on the extra lock, then got back into bed.

What had happened? I had invited this man into my room for consensual, adult sex. It was exciting at first and then some switch was turned and I wasn't OK with it anymore.

It wasn't as though I'd been raped. I remembered, though, something a woman in my book group had said, talking about a group she was counseling, women she referred to as "fresh rapes." I hated that phrase but didn't say anything at the time. To me it sounded as dehumanizing and objectifying as the rape itself. "They're feeling out of control," she had said. "The world as they understood it has suddenly changed."

I went into the bathroom and took a long, hot shower. Then I took the extra blanket from the closet and sat in the chair staring out the window, thinking of nothing. Hours passed, and I watched the skyline until the first silhouettes of buildings began to appear in the dawn light and pink-orange streaks spread across the sky.

I dressed, went down to the executive center, and worked there until it was time to take a taxi to my deposition. I didn't want to risk seeing him in the breakfast room.

I have taken the deposition, and it went well, and now I will get on the plane, and go home, storm or no storm, and see my dog. I'll try to shrug it off, like Betsy would, a story you tell after a few drinks with the girls about the guy you let pick you up in Chicago. Maybe I'll talk to the Reverend Liz at my church; she knows how to listen without instantly offering a solution.

I've always thought of myself as having good judgment with men. It occurs to me now that I've hardly exercised any judgment at all, never taking risks, never exposing myself. Here's what the live oyster feels like when it's opened: quivery, defenseless, thoroughly out of its element.

Other People's Dogs

Halfway through our thirties, my husband and I decided to leave our jobs and move to the mountains. I was working at a big-box store for thirty-five hours a week and no benefits, and I hated myself every time I pulled on my yellow pinnie and walked through the gaping maw of the loading dock out back. Each time I clocked in it was like a stamp of disapproval. I should've finished the B.A. after I graduated from St. Agatha's, should've gotten the right credentials for the better job, should've listened, at least that once, to my parents instead of rejecting all their advice wholesale. I saw myself as an artist, but lately it had seemed I had less and less energy for throwing pots.

The old joke—"What does an English major say after he graduates? 'You want fries with that?'"—seemed all too applicable to me. My version—"What is an artist who doesn't make art? A shelf-stocker."—is less catchy but was beginning to feel like my life's course.

My husband, Dan, is a solid midwesterner who can fix anything, build anything, and put together the most complicated piece of electronic equipment you could imagine. He's also dyslexic, so he didn't do too well in school. He moved south following a girlfriend who broke up with him three months later, and we met when I took a gardening workshop at the community college, both of us interested in learning to grow what we could then put up and eat. My parents weren't crazy about Dan ("Who are his people?"

my mother asked), but they grew to like the way he could repair anything they needed around the house and his willingness to get dirty and sweaty out in the yard when my mother needed a new rose-bed dug.

Once we made the decision, we started driving into the hills on weekends, scouting out territory. We saved our money, stopped going out to eat, turned down the thermostat, and dreamed through the winter. Early in March, we were driving through the Ozarks near Fayetteville and saw a sign: "Camp Kum-Ba-Yah, For Sale." An arrow pointed the way down a dirt track. It was an old Methodist summer church camp, with a main building, a screened-in meeting hall, a swimming hole, a barn, a nurse's station, and plenty of room for a big kitchen garden. Pay dirt. It was weird, but it would work. We'd start with what was there and fix it up as we went along. And the view, over a sparkling, trickling creek across to a green wooded hillside, was beautiful.

We called the number, found we could afford the price, arranged the mortgage, and planned to work on it all summer and move in come September.

The main building had a large central room with a commercial kitchen off the back. To the left and right were wings with bedrooms, presumably one wing for boys and one for girls. We figured to take one wing for ourselves, knocking out some walls for a large bedroom and living area, and get the other wing ready for friends to visit. I could take one of the outbuildings, probably the nurse's station, for a pottery studio, Dan could store his tools in the barn and maybe even have a goat and some chickens, and the meeting hall would be great for hot weather, keeping out mosquitoes while giving us a place to read and eat and hang out.

All summer, we took turns working on the main building and putting in and tending a garden. I was determined to grow and put up most of our food, supplemented by eggs, goat milk and cheese, and whatever Dan turned up in the woods. He's a good hunter, but he only kills what we can eat.

We slept on an air mattress in the big room or in a tent when the nights got hot and the inside air stuffy and stale. The creek sent up its cool breezes and lulling burbles, and we woke to birdsong.

While all this was going on, both of us happy as clams about our new life, I should say that most of our family and friends were telling us that we were crazy. What about health insurance? What about snakes? What about email and FedEx and cable TV? My mother didn't say much, devoted as she was to Being Positive with her daughters, but her face said volumes. It said, "Where Did I Go Wrong?" and "Why Can't She Be Like My Other Daughters?" and, finally, "This Must Be Dan's Idea." This last left her ambivalent, I could tell. She is very much in favor of Supporting Your Husband but she also felt that perhaps there might be some kind of marital exemption for Supporting Your Husband When He Wants To Do A Crazy Thing Like Move Out Into The Wilderness.

Both my sisters were used to me being the rebellious little sister, so they each just took me aside and promised I could stay with them if I started going stir-crazy and needed a break and/or a hot bath.

Once our friends started to believe that we were really going to do this thing, and that it might actually work, they began to ask about coming to visit. Dan and I had decided that we needed to make it through the first winter on our own and that then we could start having people in, once we'd worked out all the kinks in the system—whatever they might be—and gotten some guest rooms fixed up in the other wing. Our two cats, Beavis and Butthead (Danny's idea—I call Butthead "Little B"), had examined the premises and found them acceptable, with probably a lifetime supply of small skittery things to chase and play with and a number of warm sunny spots beneath south-facing windows. Dan had brought them home from the lumber store where he was working then. Someone had dropped off these two kittens, one coal black, the other snow white, by the dumpsters and he couldn't stand to leave them out there on the first cold night of the year.

We got a nice wood-burning stove at a salvage place, Dan fixed up the old generator, we laid in a supply of firewood for the stove and propane for the cooking range, and on a sunny day in September we moved. Despite the hard work of supporting ourselves through the winter, staying warm and fed and clean, I often fell into dreamy, slumbrous states. Never before had there been such clarity in my life, such peace. No phone to answer (we used the one at the gas station and general store five miles away), nothing much to buy, no cars or customers or television or . . . stimulation. That was it—I had come to live with so much external stimulation that I hardly knew what it felt like simply to sit and look out at the trees, follow the path of sunlight and shadow across the hill, wait for the hawk that always showed up at dusk. We could get the NPR station from Fayetteville, but I was happy to listen to it just in the evening, once the sun went down. Without smoking a single joint, I could watch a terrapin make his way across the grass for half an hour, marveling at the sturdiness of his legs, the patterning of his shell, imagining what life looked like from his one-inch-off-the-ground perspective.

I set up my wheel and began working on pots, challenging myself to accept no less than my best. I folded a lot of thrown bowls back into clumped balls, but it felt like growth, not failure. We celebrated my first firing with a bottle of wine and a skinny-dip in the creek.

Dan and I seemed more in tune, better in bed, easier with each other than we'd been in a while. When the first guests started arriving, we were the picture of relaxation, and the best kind, that earned after the virtuous work is completed.

Janice and Pete asked if they could bring their English bulldog, Jeeves. Sure, I said, lots of room for animals!

Carita and James asked about bringing their two standard poodles, Heloise and Abelard.

Susan and Cotter brought Beowulf.

Millie and Angela brought Oprah and Maya.

Jack (aka Big Jack, Jacko, Maniac Jack) brought Boner, Booger, and Pissant.

It became the summer of other people's dogs.

Although I am aware that you should be able to identify yourself as either a dog person or a cat person, I am neither. I don't dislike either felines or canines, I just don't see the point. Growing up, we never had pets because my oldest sister, Caroline, was allergic to pet dander. Well, we did have fish, but who can get attached to a fish? They either eat or are eaten.

Dan likes cats because he says they're very tidy, and he is responsible for taking them to the vet, worming them, even changing the litter box. It's one of the things I like about him, that he never pawns those chores off on me. But most of our friends seem to have dogs, and I've learned to get along with them, carefully. When I was seven a neighbor's Pekinese I was supposed to be learning to pet chomped down on my hand and held on like a Gila monster until its jaws were pried apart. I had to get a tetanus shot and three stitches, though fortunately not rabies shots. When we were kids, rabies shots were rumored to be the worst fate imaginable, apart from actually getting rabies: two weeks of painful shots—in your stomach.

But, as I say, I've learned to live with my friends' dogs, to see them as cute if slightly annoying children that never grow up. I'd never had to actually live with them, though.

The first time I walked out to the kitchen, morning-groggy in my sock feet, and stepped directly into a warm puddle of pee, I was furious—and vocal. Susan shot out of the guest room, apologizing profusely. "Beowulf's really housetrained, I promise!" she said. "Must be the new surroundings. I am so, so sorry." I ended up feeling as though I'd over-reacted. And he didn't do it again, so perhaps it was just a singular accident. The trouble was, he must have sprayed a few spots I didn't see or step in because for the next two months each new dog that arrived had to mark his spot over the last dog, ad infinitum. I investigated the relative odor-removing properties of various sprays: Ur-Out!, Ex-stink-shun, The Pee-liminator. As a last resort, one Sunday morning, scratching my flea bites, wearing my chewed-up tennis shoes (without socks, as I had just soiled my last clean pair), I called my mother. Actually took the truck, drove to the gas station, phoned her number, and was crying when she answered.

"Honey, what's wrong? Is it Dan?"

"No, Mom, no, I'm sorry. It's really no big deal, but—all these dogs!"

"Did you get bit?"

"No. They pee everywhere. All of them. I'm so tired of cleaning it up and being nice about it."

There was a silence as my mother digested the situation. "All your friends are bringing their dogs, and you don't feel you can say no, and the dogs are urinating inside, and you're being left to clean it up," she said.

"Yeah, that's it," I said, marveling, as always, at her ability to zero in on the heart of the matter. "They feel so bad when it happens that I've just stopped mentioning it," I said. "But I can't take it any longer. I really can't."

"Juney," she said, calling me by my old childhood nickname, which somehow made me feel that it was going to be OK. "First, you need some baking soda. That'll take away the smell and make them stop marking the territory. Then you need something to say. Let's try this: 'We have a lovely and secure pen where [fill in dog's name] is more than welcome to stay.' Say it after me."

Feeling silly but also not crying any more, I repeated the magic phrase. Twice. "But, Mom," I said. "We don't. Have a lovely and secure pen."

"That's what Dan is for," she replied. "He can build anything in no time."

I picked up a very expensive, very small bag of dog food at the gas station store, which had just opened, because Millie and Angela had forgotten to bring any, and headed home to talk to Dan. On the way inside I stepped in a fragrant pile of poop, strengthening my resolve. I felt that Dan would be on my side because he'd already lost two chickens, Esmerelda and Samantha, to visiting dogs that summer and because Beavis and Little B had become shadowy figures, showing up for food but otherwise finding safe, dog-free perches on beams and the tops of cabinets throughout the long summer days.

Dan measured, sawed, hammered. I cleaned, vacuumed, practiced. By the time Carly and Sam asked to come and bring their dog, Wolf Blitzer, I was ready with my mother's phrase, plus my own variations, and this is what I said:

"We have a lovely and secure pen where Wolfie is more than welcome to stay. Oh, and be sure to bring a leash for walking him—black bears have been sighted around here, and on top of that, you know those deer hunters are none too careful." Nobody need know deer season doesn't start for months.

Needs Work

I'm like those yellow flowers you see growing all along the edge of the highway—pretty and bright, but common, and trying to stay alive and grow without any fertilizer.

What I have just written is a simile, comparing two things using *like* or *as*. I didn't have time for literature when I was in high school, but now I am trying to catch up on some of the things I missed out on when all I could think about was boys, one specifically, Glenn Roberts.

Sex will make you crazy. Lust, passion, desire—you can use whatever synonyms you like, but the result is the same: in the grip of it, you will be stupider than you ever thought you could be and agree to things that a normal rational person in her right mind would never in a million years say yes to.

For instance: Glenn Roberts and I did it in his car in the back lot of the Dairy Queen (although the DQ was closed at the time), on a railroad trestle with a gully beneath us, in the bathroom at the movies, on an old couch down by the river, and even in the janitor's closet at school, with the smell of disinfectant and old mops all around and people passing by right outside the door. I didn't get off on the risk, although I think maybe Glenn did. I just could not refuse or resist those brown eyes and brawny shoulders and lips that looked like they were carved out of marble. And I didn't really want to.

It made my mother crazy, of course. She could see what I couldn't, although I think she was mostly worried about me getting knocked up and not finishing school.

I was pretty naïve then. I thought Glenn was bad in a kind of James Dean *Rebel without a Cause* way, not in a *Bonnie and Clyde* kind of way, but one day we went for a ride and stopped outside a country store and I was waiting in the car when Glenn came running out holding his side and yelling at me to scoot over and drive. It turned out he'd tried to rob the store and got shot for his trouble.

He got caught, of course. It's not that big a county. And when the dust settled I was charged with accessory to a crime, as the getaway driver, if you can believe that. Well, Glenn committed a crime, and I drove, but to this day I do not in my heart believe I was guilty of anything other than bad judgment in my choice of boyfriends. The store owner wasn't hurt at all, which is a good thing. I've met women in here who were driving the car when their no-good boyfriend killed somebody in a robbery, and they're going to be here a long time, sometimes even longer than the boyfriend. There's also a woman on death row who killed her husband and whose daughter, some kind of survivalist type, writes once a week and visits her once a month, always wearing old army fatigues.

We have a teacher who comes out from the community college three times a week. You can tell she means well, the way she tries to encourage everybody in the class, even the practically brain-dead meth heads. She was a little jumpy at first, but she's settled down, like you do in this place. She has to follow the rules—no earrings, no watch, no white clothes (we wear white), all her stuff in a clear plastic bag—but she looks like a dangly-earring kind of person to me, kind of old hippyish. She always wears shoes that are easy to slip off for shakedown, but not clogs because they're not allowed either. I could see her as a clog person, though. She doesn't wear much makeup, but I think she probably doesn't wear much anyway. She does have a wedding ring, so we know that about her, but she doesn't talk much about her personal life, probably they tell her not to, except things that don't really tell you much, like she likes to watch football and go camping, and both her grandmothers are dead.

I've thought about not going back to class. I'm not sure. I only have six weeks to go here before I probably move to work release, and I can't finish the class anyway, it has eight weeks to go. Even with her encouraging attitude, this teacher kind of bugs me, the way she seems so superior, like she knows more than we do. Which she does, about certain things, but we have our own things we know. We know about men, and how you can't trust them. About judges, who are mostly men, and how you have to please them and follow their instructions if you want to get out. About officers, and how not to cross them. About who our real friends are, now that we're inside. About the best times to take a shower and use the toilet and get to the cafeteria and smoke a cigarette. What the moon looks like through barbed wire and how it sounds when a hundred women are all asleep in the same giant room.

I was trying to write about some of this, and all she wanted to do was correct my grammar. She uses a green pen instead of a red one, like that's supposed to spare our feelings, but basically it's still like she wrote "wrong, wrong, wrong" all over the paper in green alien blood. I know how to survive here: don't speak up, don't stick out, don't make a fuss, no matter what. I never used drugs in my life but if I have to wait all morning in line to take a piss test just because somebody got something into the prison and somebody took it, I'll stand there and not complain. I remind myself that whether we are on lockdown or not really doesn't matter. If you think about it, you have nowhere to go in prison but just a different part of the prison.

She told us in advance that she marks the corrections for our own good, so that we can learn what's right and then, when we get out, we can do better for ourselves, but I think she doesn't get that if we are lucky enough to find jobs, they will be in kitchens and hotels and chicken plants, not anywhere anybody will care if we know the difference between *that* and *which* or *who* and *whom* or *If I was you* and *If I were you.*

If I were she—how's that for awkward sounding—I might be a little more careful. She keeps an eagle eye on her stuff, but it would be pretty easy to distract her and slip something into her bag. I thought about doing that. I thought about it for about twelve hours, during the so-called pork cutlet, the lumpy instant mashed potatoes, and the brown-green lima beans that were my supper, on through lying in my bed reading the latest James Patterson, and lying there later, at night, not sleeping, listening to Janine, in the bunk above me, grind her teeth in her sleep and toss and turn so her butt makes a moving lump in the mattress, like a hand in a sweatshirt, through getting up at 4 A.M. for a shower, pulling on my same crappy prison uniform and then riding in the van on my way to work in the laundry at the annex.

She had written, in big block letters across the top of my paper, where anyone could see it, NEEDS WORK. Normally I can do pretty well. Grammar isn't all that hard. Sentences are pretty easy once you get how they work. But when I wrote this one essay, I just forgot about writing correctly while I was trying to describe what it felt like to live here. If you can call it living.

And I thought it wouldn't be that hard to get some kind of contraband, pills or a joint or a knife or whatever, slip it into her bag, hope she didn't notice, and then it would get her in trouble the next time she came to teach. She'd get shook down and they'd find something. Let her know what it feels like to be unjustly accused. Assumed guilty until proven innocent.

I thought about it. And finally, pulling a load of fresh-bleached white shirts and pants out of the washer, steam rising off the clothes, the harsh but clean bleach smell in my nostrils, I thought about her big old innocent moon-face and decided I would let her stay innocent. I would finish the class, as much as I could, maybe get an early completion. After all, I'm between a rock and hard place here. (Idiom, metaphor.) But unlike the old women who came here so many years ago they hardly even remember what they were convicted of, who don't even bother to put their bad-fitting dentures in, unlike the crack whores who'll probably go right back to the life when they get out of here, unlike the retards who are doing as good as they'll ever probably do, I have hope. I want to write children's books someday. I would get married if I found a good man. I swallow my anger, let it flow out through the fingers of my right hand into my pen, let it strike the page with clean, hard words lined up like soldiers, marching across the page.

Sandra

Every weekday morning at seven, I get up, shower, feed my cats Caddy and Benjy, and walk the three blocks down to La Roche Bakery and Café, where I get a cup of coffee—OK a grande latte—and a brioche, and write for two hours. As long as the weather is bearable I sit outside at one of the tables on the outdoor patio. In the most blistering days of summer and freezing of winter, I move just inside the door, by the window, where I can still gaze out over the Arkansas River when I look up to ponder my next sentence.

A lot of people think La Roche is owned by somebody named La Roche, but it's actually a play on La Petite Roche, the original French name for the city of Little Rock. It's only a short walk from the café to the actual rock, a stone's throw, you might say.

I like writing there because it's close to home, the morning manager, Jimbo, doesn't mind how long I sit, and if I have any research questions I need to check out for the novel, I can stop by the main library, just two blocks away, on my walk home. (I don't let myself look up stuff on the web while I'm writing, plus I like old-fashioned research and its serendipities.) I work from noon to 8:00 P.M. as an aide at a facility for disturbed children. Morning writing suits me best, anyway, when my mind is fresh and uncluttered by any events of the day.

I am writing a novel about southern women. My mother frequently asks, "Ruth, you're not writing about *us*, are you?" I say of course not, but of course the answer is actually yes and no. I try to follow some writing advice I heard once, to make the characters different enough from you and the people you know so that when they need to do something you wouldn't do, you can still write that.

My girlfriend, Francine, is a Kinko's manager by day and a rock goddess by night. I'm not much of a night owl, so if we want to hang out, we have from when I get off work at 8:00 to when she goes out at 11:00 or so to listen or play. I'm short and small and have short dark hair—I tended to get mistaken for a boy, especially when I was a batgirl for the Arkansas Travelers, before I filled out a bit in adolescence. Francine is tall and slim and has long brown hair. Her arms are muscular from playing the electric guitar.

I like the balance in my life right now—working hard during the week, resting and goofing off and being with Francie on the weekends. Sometimes I sense change is in the air. But then I think I'm just being paranoid.

One of the regularities of my life right now is Sandra. The first day I met her I was sitting at my usual table at La Roche, sipping my coffee and staring over my laptop screen at the river. I noticed out of the corner of my eye that someone was moving slowly past the patio, along the wrought-iron fence that marks it off from the sidewalk. My mind was elsewhere, so she came into focus slowly as well. An old lady. In very bright clothes with lots of scarves. Tall. Erect. Wild gray hair that looked like the unpruned olive trees I had once seen on a summer trip to Greece. A bit . . . off. I looked up at her, and she looked at me. I smiled, helloed.

She said, "Hello, darlin'" back.

Then I could tell she was homeless. Something about her looked hungry.

I hate for anyone or anything to be hungry. I had bought a muffin for a snack at work and it was sitting in a little white sack on the table, so I offered it to her.

"Muffin?"

"What kind?" she said.

"Cranberry orange."

"Yes, then, thank you." She paused. "But I have to give you something for it." She rummaged in her pocket, pulled out a silver button, placed it on the table with her right hand, picked up the muffin sack with her left, and walked on. "Ta," she said over her shoulder, like some aging British actress departing a tea table.

The next day it was a bran muffin, the next carrot-walnut bread. We spoke only a little until the fourth day, when she approached with misery written in the lines of her forehead, the weight of a worrisome world on her shoulders.

"Bad things are going to happen," she said. "Darlin', it's getting worse. I got second-hand smoke in my lungs, I got free radicals in my blood, there's heavy metals in the water and hormones in the beef and antibiotics in the chicken and microwaves in the air and PCBs in the beautiful earth that birthed us. They're making everything extinct including me. Bad things are going to happen. Dirty bombs. Alar. Inoculation injections. Cell phones causing brain tumors. Chemicals in your clothes, your sheets, your sofa. West Nile, Ebola, superflu. I'm superfluous, are you?" The restlessness in her body seemed to make it hard for her to stand still. Her arms traced patterns in the air, her legs moved like a runner's at a stoplight.

"My name is Ruth," I said. "What's yours?"

She looked at me as though she had just seen me. "Sandra," she said. "You can call me Sandra. But I will just call you Darlin'."

Then she put a pecan, mottled light brown with dark specks, onto the table, and picked up the bag containing two whole wheat scones. She was shaking her head as she walked away, and I heard again the words "bad things."

Jimbo tells me that she comes to the back door on Saturdays and Sundays for day-old goods, but that she won't take anything with "refined sugars," which includes cinnamon rolls, bear claws, even *pain au chocolat* (my personal favorite). She doesn't exchange anything for them. Perhaps, in her system, day-old doesn't require it.

Francie tells me that she has seen her walking all over town, striding along in her floral skirt and bright tops and multiple scarves and tennis shoes, as though she were on her way to keep an appointment, and that she sometimes comes into Kinko's and makes copies of her poems, a few of which she has shown me.

Our conversation started out with her sally, "You a writer?"

I dread this question. "Yes," I said. "I'm writing a novel."

Usually I then get asked what it's about, and unless I am in an especially forgiving and kind mood, I respond, "It's a postmodern multi-generational matriarchal southern novel spanning three centuries and two continents, the bastard love-child of William Faulkner and Alice Walker." That usually shuts them up.

But Sandra was only getting to the part of the conversation that concerned her. "I got fired for writing poetry," she said. "At least, that's what the official reason was. But I think it was for telling the truth. Want to see my poems?"

I did not. But I said yes. She produced several wrinkled, perhaps coffee-stained sheets of paper.

"Keep them," she said grandly, with a wave of her hand. "Plenty more where those came from."

I put them in my bag and read them when I got home.

The first:

> you may someday find me
> high up in a mad tree
> don't fear
> i'll clear
> the sky

The second:

> a quiet mind
> keeps its own company
> alone

the roan horse
is no friend of mine

And the third:
    tell the world
    you're a wildflower
    no one cares
    tell them
    you're a god
    then they'll listen

I mentioned the poems to the art therapist at work. She asked me to describe Sandra, and when I did, a smile came to her face.

"Oh yeah," she said. "I used to work at the shelter doing art workshops on the weekends for homeless families. She'd drop by and sit and write her poems. I think she came mostly for the paper." She finished putting the crayon boxes away on a low shelf and stood up. "One of the social workers at the shelter says she has a sister who helps her when she can, with a shower or some food or clothes, but she refuses to sleep inside. Thinks it's too dangerous. She prefers her camp in that little triangle of woods at the intersection of I-430 and Rodney Parham. She wrote some nice stuff, though. I hadn't thought about her in a while." Then she went back to straightening up.

I have a big glass bowl in my apartment where I keep all the things Sandra has traded for breakfast: a variety of small stones, some round, some oval, some like very small pancakes, that would be good for skipping; a mussel shell from the river; a pine cone; a shiny Phillips-head screw; a bluejay feather; an old-fashioned key; a one-inch-square fragment of mirror; a snail shell; a magnolia cone with bright red seeds; a yellow and milky-white swirled marble; a buffalo nickel; a backless pearl stud earring; a wooden spool for thread; the Scrabble letter "C"—she seemed especially pleased with this one; a bright lime-green plastic ring with a compartment on top that opened and closed; several shards of glazed pottery, from plates, perhaps; a six-inch piece of sky-blue plastic-coated wire, bent into a circle; a bright-yellow Hot Wheels Corvette, fairly scratched up; an army-green plastic soldier; a locust shell, its thin brown carapace a perfect mask of the living creature; a small chunk of blue glass; a wheatie penny; a hot-pink golf ball; a new pencil, unsharpened; a Corona bottle cap, like a small golden sun; and an Arkansas quarter from the state commemorative series.

I fancy that I serve as her reliquary, the place she keeps all the treasures she can't carry with her. Trading the treasures for a muffin, she keeps things even between us and keeps the treasures safe.

Yesterday morning I arrived at La Roche, as usual, after mailing a funny card to my grandmother, who's on dialysis, and went to the counter for coffee and brioche and something for Sandra. Kara, who just started working there, said she'd bring it out to me. When she came outside, she said, "Hey, did you hear about the homeless woman who got hit by a car last night, just down the street by the Capital Hotel? Sad thing. She died."

"Was it Sandra?" I asked her, my heart suddenly pounding. "The woman who comes by here every day?"

She shrugged. She was too new to recognize the local homeless regulars. "An old lady, they said. The driver was on his cell phone and didn't see her." She went back in, shivering with the new autumn coolness of October.

I sat staring at the screen of my laptop. The words blurred, and tears ran hot down my cheeks. Damn, I thought. Not Sandra. Damn.

I took a sip of coffee and burned my tongue. Chewed at a bite of brioche and almost choked on it. I didn't think I would get much writing done, so I closed up the laptop. When I looked at the little white sack next to it I started to cry again.

I heard someone walking up, slowly recognized it as a familiar walk, and looked up.

"Sandra!" I yelled.

She looked at me like I was crazy. "Hey darlin'."

"I thought you died. I thought you got hit by a car. They said a woman got hit by a car last night," I blurted.

"Oh, that," she said, twisting one end of a scarf in her hand. "I heard about that. She was new. I've seen her, but I don't know her. She forgot the number one rule of survival: Pay attention."

Then she looked at me again, noticed my drying tears. Her eyes softened from their usual fierceness and anxiety, and she gave me the first look of compassion and consideration I had seen on her face. She looked at me as a mother might, or as a friend. She looked right into my eyes and I saw the abysses where she lived.

"Oh, darlin'," she said, her feet dancing with their wish to move on, her hands worrying the hem of her sweater. "It's a world of pain. You can't get too attached. I tell you, it's a world of pain."

Then she carefully placed a tiny silver goblet fashioned from a chewing-gum wrapper on the table, picked up the sack, and walked away.

The Other Grandparents

My mother only this week told me the story of when Truman Capote came to her seventh birthday party. He didn't come to Arkansas, where she grew up—not ever, that I know of. She was visiting cousins in Monroeville, Alabama, and, as the visit fell on her birthday, they threw her a party with the neighbor children in attendance. In a picture from that day my mother showed me, the girls are in frilly white dresses with anklet socks and sandals or patent-leather shoes. Mr. Capote is in the picture as well, speaking to my grandmother, who at that time of course was a pretty, still-young woman in a becoming dress. My mother's first cousin Jenny was a poised and precocious child, which makes me wonder whether Truman Capote got his inspiration for "Children on Their Birthdays" from that party. He, too, must have been visiting cousins in Monroeville. Thankfully, unlike Miss Bobbitt in the story, no one was hit by the six o'clock bus that day, but something did happen, something my mother both knows and does not know. What she knows is that Mr. Capote said something extraordinary to her mother and that she was never quite the same afterward. What she does not know, because she never found the right moment to ask in the years before her mother died, is what he said, or why he was moved to say it. It seems possible to me that this black-and-white almost chiaroscuro photo was taken just as he was speaking to her and that it captured her psychic state. Her head seems light, fuzzy, almost immaterial, not a lack of focus or a flaw in the equipment but a true picture of how she felt. She is half-turned, in profile, while he is facing the camera, though with dark sunglasses that hide his eyes. He looks annoyed at the photographer or perhaps just at the glare of the afternoon light and the emptiness of his highball glass.

My mother, Susanna, said that her mother, Lucy, had taken her down to Alabama on the train, a long journey and not direct, to get away from her father for a little while. "She would take these breaks periodically," my mother told me, "when his goodness just got to be too much for her." My grandfather—named Franklin, after FDR—was ever patient, kind, temperate, helpful, easygoing, understanding, and loving. For a woman of my grandmother's temperament, who needed to kick up her heels, kick off the traces, and in general just kick back every once in a while, his saintliness made her feel shallow and selfish, so when she felt a little evil coming on, she'd pack up a suitcase and take my mother to visit some cousins, of whom she had plenty, and she would smoke and drink and gossip and cackle until she got it out of her system and could once again appreciate the many fine qualities of my grandfather.

After this trip, though, after whatever Mr. Capote said to her, she began, occasionally, to talk to herself in the morning while she made coffee, along the lines, my mother said, of someone arguing with herself: "Well, why don't you? But what good would it do now? Well, you won't ever know if you don't try, will you? Water under the bridge, my dear, water . . . under . . . bridge."

On the day she died, many years later, she uttered a cryptic statement that made my mother wonder further: "He was right—I wasn't as bad as I thought I was. That was true." Or "Tru." Of course it wasn't possible to know.

The birthday party was in July. They returned to Arkansas for the long, hot, lazy dog days when summer is ending and everything is dry but autumn has not yet come. School started the weekend after Labor Day, and the next weekend Lucy announced to Susanna that they were going on a picnic, and wouldn't that be fun. My grandfather was helping somebody with something that day and so did not go with them. Lucy packed a heavy picnic basket and put it in the back seat of the Chevrolet, and Susanna got in the front, buckled her seatbelt across her lap, the metal buckle already hot from the day's sun, and they pulled out of the driveway.

To Susanna's question about where they were going for their picnic, Lucy would say only that it would be a surprise in more ways than one. She seemed nervous but at the same time determined, her permed hair brushed high off her forehead, her lipstick making a red flag of her lips, her manicured nails tapping a repeated drum roll on the steering wheel at stoplights.

They drove out of town along the highway for several miles then turned off on a county road my mother didn't know. The road curved and rose, crossing dappled shadows of leaves and passing few houses.

Just about the time Susanna was about to have to ask her mother to stop so she could go, by the side of the road behind a bush if necessary, her mother said, "Morrison, 6300 County Road 14 West. That has to be it," and pulled into a driveway marked by a tilting, scarred mailbox, a hand-lettered "Keep Out" sign, and an old tire in which a few yellow and orange marigolds, grown leggy and sparse, eked out their lives.

My mother's part of the script was predictable. "We're stopping here? For a picnic?"

Several dogs of indeterminate breed came out from their dirt beds under a large privet hedge and began barking furiously, keeping them in the car.

Lucy looked at Susanna. "Do not, repeat, do not tell your father that we came here. Do you understand?"

"Yes ma'am."

"We are here to visit your grandparents. Your *other* grandparents. I thought it was about time. Now mind your manners and don't embarrass me in front of my in-laws."

This was the first my mother, Susanna, had heard of her father's parents. Until then, it just hadn't come up.

The dogs had retreated somewhat and when Lucy and Susanna got out of the car they barked but without real enthusiasm.

"Don't look them in the eye and they won't bother us," said Lucy, taking the picnic basket from the back seat.

More privet hedge grew in random sproutings around the house, and on the screen door a patch of screen had come loose and flapped listlessly in the dull breeze.

Lucy knocked. A minute passed during which time small sounds came from inside, as of someone trying to move quietly, and a curtain twitched very slightly. Finally the door was opened by a scrawny but wiry woman, brows furrowed in protective defense of her home. She stood, silent, waiting for her visitors to speak first.

"Ruby?" said Lucy. "It's me, Lucy. And I've brought your granddaughter, Susanna."

The woman's deep smoker's wrinkles went suddenly from frown to wide smile, then she clapped her hand over her mouth. "Haven't put my partials in yet! But Lucy, what a nice surprise. I thought you was some government lady from town. Come in, come in. Susanna, aren't you big?" And then, over her shoulder, "Hiram, you won't believe who's here!"

A sound came from behind her, the grunt of someone heaving himself up. As they entered the house, Hiram came forward. He was a fat man of the old-fashioned kind, pants pulled up over his round belly and held in place by suspenders, so that he resembled an egg with human features and clothes painted onto it.

His face, too, opened into a smile as he recognized Lucy. "Well, if it ain't my daughter-in-law! And this is your girl? Franklin's girl? Susanna? Honey, come over here and give your old granddaddy some sugar."

Susanna presented herself and kissed his proffered cheek. He smelled slightly smoky and dusty, like an old blanket from the attic.

"Ain't she pretty? And Lucy, you're a sight for sore eyes."

They sat down in the living room, a smallish and cluttered room redolent of smoke, cabbage, dog, and Pine Sol. It was a not unpleasant smell, my mother says. She sat quietly, taking in the room, while the grown-ups talked, then she remembered she had to pee.

"Excuse me, may I use the toilet please?" she asked, using her best manners.

Ruby smiled. "You sure may, but it's out back. Don't mind the dogs—they won't hurt you. But bang around a bit once you get inside to scare off any snakes." She smiled in a way that might be joking or might not. Susanna didn't know her well enough to say.

She didn't want to go after hearing about the out back and the snake part, but her mother was looking at her in a way that reminded Susanna of her promise not to embarrass her mother in front of her in-laws, and she was still young enough to worry about having an accident if she didn't go, so she walked out the front door and around the back to where a small, unpainted outbuilding stood. She lifted up the wooden latch and banged on the wall to scare the snakes. For the first time in her life she sat down on a hole cut out of a board and, after a minute of tense waiting, let loose. It sounded different from the pleasant sound going in the toilet made, both farther down and duller, and when she was finished and looked for toilet paper there were only neatly cut squares of newsprint, which she used and dropped down into the dark hole as well. She had been taught always to wash her hands afterwards but saw nowhere to wash up, so she went back inside the house and rejoined the adults.

" . . . and he stays so busy with church work and Rotary activities and so on, he just barely has a moment to himself," her mother was saying.

So they had been talking about her father while she was gone.

"But I thought," Lucy said, shifting to a brighter register as she saw Susanna returning, "I should just bring Susanna along whether he could come or not, not even bother him with asking, so here we are! Oh, and I brought us a picnic. I thought maybe we could all eat it together. In here," she added, to make clear that she did not intend for them to go out into the yard.

The picnic basket held more than enough for the three adults and one child—ham, bread, potato salad, devilled eggs, lemon squares, apples, and a tub of chicken salad they didn't even touch. As soon as they finished, Lucy put all the perishables into the old squat refrigerator that sagged into the kitchen's linoleum "so that it won't spoil," had Susanna take the basket to the car, and then conveniently forgot to retrieve the rest of the food when they left.

As they were saying their goodbyes outside, Lucy said, "Oh, I left my pocketbook on the couch," and when she came back out she had a slight smile, a secret smile Susanna had not seen before.

"Well, bye y'all," said Ruby. "We sure was happy to see you. Come back again soon." She and Hiram waved as Lucy turned the car around then headed back to the house. They were not the kind to keep waving until you were out of sight, apparently. As the car reached the highway, Susanna saw Ruby come running out of the house with an envelope in her hand, looking peeved.

"Mama, it's Grandma," Susanna said, looking out the back window. "I think she wants us to stop."

"Never mind," said Lucy. "I just left a little something for them. Now turn around and put your bottom on the seat."

On future visits—and there were several that fall that could be called picnic visits, as long as the weather held—Lucy became more devious about leaving money behind. She would give Susanna a check for twenty dollars and ask her to leave it on the mantel or in the pocket of Ruby's housedress or under her cigarette pack. But, she said, "Just don't leave it under the Lemon Pledge or it might take her months to find it."

My mother told me that she came to think of Ruby and Hiram as her secret grandparents. Her mother told her simply that her father and his parents had had some kind of falling out and that Lucy would tell him at the right time, but until then it might just be best not to mention it. It would be a nice surprise for him when she told him, and Susanna ought to know her grandparents, said Lucy, seeing as they were the only ones she had living. Lucy's parents were by all accounts lovely people whom everyone still missed. They had died within a year of each other, her mother of cancer, her father of influenza, when Lucy was in her twenties. They had left Lucy with a small inheritance, enough to ensure her independence when she needed it, but somewhat "adrift on the seas of life" as she liked to put it. My grandfather was her anchor, though sometimes he may have seemed like a ball and chain.

Susanna was to discover that she had secret cousins as well as secret grandparents. One Saturday when they arrived, there was an unfamiliar car in the gravel driveway, an older model two-tone Chevrolet with faded paint.

"Ah!" said Lucy in her bright voice. "More family!"

They hauled the large picnic basket, once again packed full, inside the house, where Susanna met her father Franklin's sister, her Aunt Bunny, so-called because she was born on Easter. Bunny had twin boys, Cletus and Clay, currently out in the woods somewhere trying to catch a snake. That first day they would torment my mother, in the way of boys, teasing her until she cried, with the threat of making her eat dirt. The next time, she wore her pointy-toed shoes and kicked each one hard in the shins before they knew what had happened, after which a respectful détente prevailed.

Cletus and Clay did not so much eat as inhale, and Bunny would issue mild, ineffectual warnings to them that merely slowed their progress as their pig-like eyes registered on her and then went back to surveying what was left to eat. After the first time with the boys, Lucy removed several packages from the basket in advance and hid them in the refrigerator or cupboards, out of the direct line of the boys' voraciousness.

Christmas came and went, and with cold weather their visits grew few, but they picked up again in the spring. One warm Saturday morning in May they had made their visit and were halfway home when Susanna became aware of a thudding sound. She looked at her mother who was clearly noticing it too but pretending not to, as though it might go away.

"Damn!" she said, giving the rarely said word at least two syllables, heavily diphthonged. "You didn't hear that, Susanna," she added parenthetically. "Damn damn damn damn damn. Or that."

She pulled off on the shoulder in the shadow of a hillside, got out, and verified what she knew to be true: the presence of a flat tire, or, put another way, the absence of air in the right rear tire.

"Well, Susanna, your mother does not change tires, so we will just have to wait for a good Samaritan. How ironic."

They sat in the car with the windows down, ate the two slightly crumbled brownies left in the basket, shared a warm Coke, and sat some more.

"Mama," said Susanna.

"What," said Lucy.

"Why doesn't Daddy visit Mama Ruby and Papa Hiram?"

"He's just mad about some things that happened a long time ago. He'll get over it."

"What things?" Susanna's eyes, and her mother's, were both closed as they rested their heads on the back of the car seat and held still for the little breeze coming in the windows. It was easier to talk about such things with your eyes closed.

"If I tell you, you can't tell your father, or let him know you know. Are you grown up enough to do that?"

Susanna nodded. Who would turn back now? Even with their eyes closed, her mother knew she had nodded her agreement. The breeze blew a stray hair across Susanna's cheek, and the world seemed to have let out its breath.

My mother said this is the story Lucy told her:

"You can see they don't have a lot of money now. Well, they had even less then. Everybody was hurting because of the Great Depression. Somehow or another, Ruby got an idea in her head. And when Ruby gets an idea, watch out.

"She piled the kids in the car and started driving. After about an hour they reached a town, and she drove onto Main Street and parked. Of course the kids had been asking what they were doing, and she had put them off, but after she parked the car she told them they were going to play a little game, a Christmas game—did I say it was Christmastime, and cold?—and that the children, Franklin, Eddie, and Bunny were to keep their mouths shut except for yes ma'am and no ma'am.

"They walked along the sidewalk, past tantalizing displays of toys in the department store window, to the local café, where they sat in a booth and she ordered a cup of coffee and one piece of pie with four forks. The waitress paused then put in the order at the counter. Ruby put her head in her hands. Her shoulders began to shake slightly.

"'Mama, what's wrong?' Franklin asked.

"She spread her fingers open so that he could see her right eye, and she winked. At that moment, Franklin says, he thought she'd gone crazy.

"The coffee and pie came, four forks, and she straightened up, brushed at her eyes, and thanked the waitress.

"'Everything all right, ma'am?'

"'Oh, yes, thank you,' said Ruby. 'It's just—well, this world is a vale of tears, ain't it, and we'll all be better in the sweet by and by.'

"The waitress paused. 'How 'bout I bring these children a glass of milk each, no charge?'

"Ruby began to pretend-weep again, softly, and this set off Eddie and Bunny.

"'You are so kind. Thank you. I'm not usually like this, but I've been to see my mother in the hospital in Little Rock, and somebody stole money from my purse in the waiting room while we was all sleeping, and their daddy has had to take work down in Texas . . .'

"By this time she had attracted the attention of several of the other diners, and by the time she left the café they had been given a full meal, more pie, gas money, and an invitation for the children to pick out a toy each at the department store.

"Franklin, as the oldest, was mortified. Bunny never had much going on between her ears and just went along. And your Uncle Eddie, whom you haven't met and I hope never will, just blossomed into his role—a born con man.

"On the drive home Ruby explained that people needed to feel the Christmas spirit, that she was doing them a favor by giving them a chance to help others less fortunate than themselves.

"Franklin took his toy and gave it to a little colored boy down the road. He tried to forget the whole thing, but the next year she did it again, in a different town. She changed up the story as it pleased her—her mother had died, her husband was in prison, one of the children needed treatment for scoliosis (Eddie particularly enjoyed stories in which he could play the lead). Each time, Franklin tried to get out of going, and each time his father forced him into the car. His evident misery actually worked to Ruby's advantage."

Susanna had been listening quietly the whole time, but she had a question that needed asking. "But Papa Hiram? Didn't he care? Wasn't he embarrassed?"

"I'm afraid not," her mother said. "Hiram is lazy as an old dog, always has been. He thought Ruby was 'right clever' to come up with her little scheme.

"One Christmas, when Franklin was thirteen and nearly big enough to resist his father, vowing to himself this was his last time, they went through the usual rigmarole and were in the process of being taken pity on by the local folk. Ruby decided to up the ante, just to make things more interesting for herself, and asked the café owner if she might possibly place a very quick call to her mother in the hospital, just to let her know they were going to be all right. He agreed, reluctantly— long-distance calls used to be a big deal, undertaken only for major life events like a birth or a death—and she called Hiram from the back office. Somehow or another the owner had gotten suspicious of her, and he picked up the phone on the counter and listened in.

"As she came out of the back, sniffling a little for effect, he met her and blocked her way. Franklin saw his mother's face go momentarily white before she recovered herself. The owner took her by the elbow, gently but firmly, and guided her to the booth to gather up the children and then out the door of the café, as she waved her thanks to the patrons. 'No charge!' he was saying as they walked outside, smiling so that he seemed to be wishing her a Merry Christmas and a safe journey. What he really said was, 'Lady, I'm not going to ruin people's Christmas by exposing you as a fraud, plus there's your children to consider, but if I ever see you or hear of you pulling this stunt again, I'll call the police on you, children or not, Christmas or not.'

"Your daddy fumed all the way home, humiliated, vowing to leave that family behind him and never return, which he did at age sixteen. Even though he ended up only thirty miles away from them, it might as well be a thousand."

"That's pretty bad, Mama," said Susanna.

"I know. They're not really very good people. They're just family. And family shouldn't be strangers to one another."

Just then the sheriff's car pulled up behind them. When the sheriff got to the window, he smiled. "Why Mrs. Jones! What're you doing out here?"

"Oh, Sheriff Clements, thank goodness you're here. I was trying to show Susanna that waterfall everybody talks about, but not being from here I got totally turned around and lost, and then we had a flat. I'm so glad to see a friendly face."

The sheriff bent to look at the tire and came back to the window. "Looks like you picked up a nail somewhere. I'll change it out for you and then you can get it to the garage."

Lucy thanked him effusively and asked him if he could possibly not mention it to Franklin, as she felt so foolish having gotten lost.

"Well, all right. But you be careful next time and get your directions straight. There's some rough folks out there in these woods, some of 'em just as soon rob you or shoot at you as look at you."

Lucy took the car to the garage when they got into town, and they walked home. When she told Franklin later, at supper, that she'd had a flat tire on the highway, she didn't say where and he didn't ask. This is how Susanna learned about the sin of omission. Later, when she was grown and had become my mother, she'd learn that when someone lets such an omission alone, it's because they are afraid of the answer their question might bring. She learned that with me, and she still blames herself for not asking, as though that would've kept me from developing a taste for wrong-side-of-town dives and pretty, heartless men who make you feel like a movie star one day and a smoked-out cigarette butt the next.

Susanna was a good child. She didn't like to lie, and her soul was at peace only when everyone around her was happy and harmonious. She loved to draw pictures of herself, Lucy, and Franklin, all smiling, in front of their house. One sunny Saturday morning she was lying on her stomach in her bedroom drawing and coloring when her father walked by the door and stopped to visit. Susanna had been working on Ruby's hair, which the silver crayon did not get quite right, and she was half in her own world of seeing and imagining.

"Who are you drawing?" he said. He was an awkward but loving father, and he wanted to show interest.

"Grandma Ruby and Grandpa Hi—" Susanna, of course, realized that she had accidentally given away their secret, and she froze, silent.

"Oh," said Franklin. "Well, keep drawing then."

She heard him walking down the hall to the kitchen where her mother was preparing lunch. The swinging door closed, its hinge squeaking.

Minutes passed, and she didn't hear anything, so she walked quietly down the hall and listened. There was a gap between the door and frame, so she put her eye to the cream-painted wood and peeked in. Her parents were sitting at the kitchen table facing each other, both of them in profile to her.

"I'm sorry, Franklin," Lucy was saying. "I should have told you. I just didn't want a fight. I thought Susanna should know them, and that she could handle it, but I shouldn't have made her keep a secret."

Her father looked tired. "To tell the truth, I'm sort of relieved. I thought something was up, and I was afraid it was something worse."

"Franklin! I wouldn't take Susanna if I were doing something like that." Seeing how it sounded, she added, "I wouldn't *do* something like that, period."

"OK. But why now? What made you decide to go now?"

Susanna had wondered that, too, but the ways of adults were mysterious.

"She called me," said Lucy. "Last summer. After we got back from Monroeville. Said she wanted to meet her grandchild, her only granddaughter. Drop by any time, she said, and would I mind bringing something for lunch, a little chicken or ham, as they were a little short this month. So I did take a picnic, like I said, but we just ate it inside. And I started leaving a little money each time, along with the leftovers from the picnic."

"You what?" Franklin said. "You what?"

Susanna began to worry that they would really fight. Her father lowered his head, put a hand to his brow, closed his eyes, and sighed deeply.

Her mother bit her plump red bottom lip.

When Franklin looked up he was smiling and shaking his head. "I've been sending her money every month since I was eighteen years old, all through our marriage, sent a money order yesterday. That old woman is *still* running her cons. I don't suppose she mentioned that to you?"

Seeing the question on Lucy's face, he said, "I know, I should have told you. I'm sorry. I was embarrassed about my sorry family and I didn't want to talk about it. So, she played us both for fools."

Susanna watched as they looked at each other for a long moment, each set of eyes a mirror to the other's.

"Fools in love," said Lucy.

He leaned across the table to kiss her, and Susanna tiptoed back to her room, soul calm. The visits continued, but no longer secretly.

My mother told me all this sitting next to my hospital bed, occasionally leaning over to give me sips of ice water from an articulated straw. "So much like your grandmother," she was saying, as I drifted back to sleep, her hand stroking my hair.

When I woke up, she was out of the room, gone to the cafeteria, I presumed, for coffee to fuel her vigil. I realized I was thirsty again and reached for my cup.

The minute I shifted in bed, my two broken ribs sent out warning flashes of pain, hot slivers in my sides. What a stupid, ridiculous, embarrassing, wasteful thing to do, drunkenly running off the road into a ditch, missing the turnoff to the driveway of the City Limits Bar and Grill in search of the latest pretty man I'd fallen too hard for, all the while telling myself what a free spirit I was, so unconventional and daring. It had been a year and a half since I'd finished college, and though I had gainful employment it was hardly what I'd dreamed of as an art major. Was this why my friends got married, to avoid the awful aloneness and disappointment of post-college life? Or even, like Karen, stay with a loser like Joel, just to be with *somebody*?

My brain clearing a little from the pain, I thought about the story. Why had she never told me that one? I thought I knew them all—the donkey in the back yard, the cigarettes taped behind the toilet, the red-headed twins who joined the circus, the church bazaar kleptomaniac, the lost letter from Great-Uncle Jack that literally fell out of the sky one Fourth of July.

Last words. Oscar Wilde's *bon mot* as he turned to the hideous wallpaper: "One of us has to go." Lucy's: "I wasn't as bad as I thought I was."

Ah, sweet Susanna. All of her stories had a message, and even in my state of fuzzy-headed self-pity I could see this one.

I could hear her voice now in the hallway, speaking to the nurse, thanking her on my behalf.

Maybe she was right, that I was like my grandmother. It would be a while, I thought, before I could know for sure.

III

String-up

I don't even know why I'm thinking about it, to be honest. It's not like I think about it hardly ever. Or like it's the worst thing I ever did. I've done worse, believe me. Not that I like to think about that, either. Besides, focus on the positive, right? I'm not one of those live-in-the-past kind of people. Ask anybody. I'm a live-in-the-moment kind of girl. No regrets.

So I guess it's the class reunion packet I got in the mail today that got me thinking about it. Who'll be there and who won't. Who's married and who isn't. I'm not, but I look great. I may be on the far side of forty but I take care of myself—nails, hair, skin. I've only gained eight pounds since graduation. And the girls still look great in a tank top, no implants or lifts required. I'd have fewer lines if I stopped smoking, but I've cut way down, and I can't give up all my vices, now can I? Of course it would be nice to be married again, not to an asshole like the last time but maybe to a nice guy, the kind of guy who mows the lawn without being nagged. I can even imagine being interested in those guys I wouldn't have given the time of day to in college, the kind of cute, nerdy guys who studied a lot and were too shy to ask me out anyway. They've probably all got good salaries and nice cars and homes now, and some of them are bound to be single, or at least divorced. So maybe I'll go. I've got nothing to be ashamed of.

I haven't kept up with that many people, just a couple of girlfriends

who were roommates in my suite. Once a year we take a trip together—
Vegas, New York, the Caymans, sometimes a cruise—and drink too
much and talk the whole time and flirt with other women's husbands,
just to remind ourselves we used to be bad girls.

I wasn't a slut or anything, but I did sow my wild oats in those years.
Unlike some of those brainy girls in my dorm, I *like* guys, and I'm not
afraid of them either. Women could do their daughters a big favor by telling them that *they're* in charge: guys want it, we have it, and as long as
we take care of ourselves, we run the game. My mom still has my dad
wrapped around her little finger, always has.

My senior year I was dating Steve Kaplan, a pre-med student who had
aced his MCATS and was making up for lost time. His best friend was
Billy Bates (Steve called him "Master," ha-ha), and the two of them ruled
their dorm and gave parties that lasted until dawn down in the basement,
where you couldn't see outdoors or whether it was light anyway.

One warm Tuesday night in spring, when you could smell the fresh-
cut grass through the open windows, the fireflies were blinking in the
trees, and the last thing you wanted to be doing was studying for sociol-
ogy class, we all heard horns honking and guys yelling, and when we
looked out our windows there was a line of cars with their lights on driving into the horseshoe-shaped parking lot by the women's dorms. I for
one thanked God for a break in the boredom. I'd been about to quit and
paint my toenails, anyway.

I could hear them yelling "String-up, string-up, string-up." I knew
what that meant, and so did my suitemates Chris and Paula. "Whoo-
hoo, party!" I heard Chris yell from the other room. "String-up, girls!"

Looking down from our second-floor window I could see the two
other dorms to my right and directly across from me, girls looking out
of their windows and lights going out, the better to see outside. In the
grass strip down the center of the parking lot was a small gazebo with a
bench that nobody ever used because it was too public. All the cars' headlights were turned on the gazebo, and five or six guys, Steve and Billy

leading the pack, of course, were carrying another guy toward it in his underwear.

The string-up is a big tradition at my college, kind of like a ritual, like maybe a coming-of-age ritual in some of those tribes? The way it works is, a guy is stripped down to his tighty-whities and padlocked to the gazebo with a chain through them, so the only way he can escape is by getting buck-naked in front of the girls' dorms and making a dash for it. It was a hoot to watch.

Usually the guy's buddies followed along and brought a towel for him to wrap around himself, once he'd made the dash, and one time a guy just dropped his drawers and then did a little *dance* before he walked, very slowly, back to his dorm. I have to say, he gave us a look at the goods, and they were pretty impressive. But that one was a lot less fun—he sort of took the excitement out of it by not being embarrassed.

Sometimes they'd pick freshmen who were too big for their britches, no pun intended, and sometimes guys who just wouldn't fit in or had broken the rules in some way or other. It was all in good fun, I mean it would've been worse to be ignored, I would think.

But this one guy was just too weird. I think he was probably a fag. Wore a silk dressing gown like frigging *Masterpiece Theatre* in the dorm, smoked a cigarette with a holder, combed stuff into his hair to slick it back. His parents had put one strike against him already by naming him Randolph, but he was the one who insisted on being called by his full name, instead of Randy or even Dolph. So Randolph was just not fitting in, and the guys decided he needed a little lesson.

His skin was totally white, I mean fish-belly white, almost as white as his jockeys. He stood there looking down toward the parking lot driveway, into the dark, as though some help might be coming for him, but really he didn't have any friends, so he was pretty much stuck there.

The guys kept yelling, "String-up! string-up! string-up!" but then it shifted to "Sally! Sally! Sally!" with Steve starting and then leading the chant, with my name. Chris and Paula were all, "Ooh, Sally, they're calling your name," so I checked myself out in the mirror and went down the stairs and out the door.

"Hey baby," Steve said. "Why not show ole Randolph a good time, let him see what he's missing?"

I gave Steve a big kiss and walked on over to where Randolph was chained to the gazebo. He had slid down and was sitting on the grass.

"Hey, Randolph," I said. "Stand up and talk to me. Maybe I can help."

He stood up, like I knew he would.

I leaned in close to him, my chest pressing up against his. Then I walked my hand down his chest and ran my finger just under the elastic of his shorts. He started breathing heavy despite himself, and I knew I had him.

"What's up, Randy?" I said. "Come on out and play, why don't you? They're just having a good time."

"Leave me alone," he said. "Bitch."

I stroked him just once before walking away to show everyone what a big boner he had, there for all the world to see, then walked over to Steve and leaned in. "Maybe he's not a fag after all, or do I just have superpowers?"

Steve laughed.

Some dorm snitch must have called security because just then the campus police drove up and all the guys melted away and jumped in their cars and got out of there as fast as they could, leaving Randolph chained to the gazebo.

Since I couldn't really get away I talked to security like I was trying to help him. They turned their headlights on him, got some cutters out of the trunk and got him loose. By then all the girls had pretty much gone back to studying. He wasn't going to run, so there was really nothing to see.

The last I saw of him he was getting into the security pickup truck. He was gone the next day, totally moved out of his room, all his little things packed up and gone. When I heard about it, I felt kind of bad. Kind of responsible. Steve said he never would've fit in anyway, and then we went and drank some beer and fooled around in Steve's room and I stopped thinking about it, mostly.

Until now, when I was thinking about who would be there, and who wouldn't. And if Randolph by some chance were there, which he wouldn't be since he wasn't a graduate and probably never wanted to see the place again, what he would say to me. What I would say to him. I could say we didn't really know what we were doing, but really we did. I could say I was sorry, but what good is sorry after twenty-five years. I could say I had tried to be a better person after that, but really I haven't. It's a tough world out there, and you're either a winner or a loser. At least, that's what I've always thought.

Residue

The thing you notice first when you walk into a hotel room is the smell, different for each one. When I worked at the Catfish Cabin, my nose became so used to that fried fish smell I didn't even smell it anymore after a while. At first, I knew how my clothes reeked after a shift, but later, I stopped noticing, until my husband would say, "Why don't you change out of those work clothes?"

But each hotel room bears a different smell after a person has left it. Sometimes it's easy—cologne, perfume, a whiff of someone's chosen scent. Other times it smells like their shampoo, and the air is moist with a recently taken shower. People leave food smells behind, of hamburgers, fried chicken, pizza, but also of apples, bananas, oranges. I think of those as the healthy eaters. There are diapers, of course, but having three kids of my own I don't mind those, especially since they haven't had the chance to sit for long. I can smell if someone snuck in their little pet dog or if they had a few beers or some expensive whiskey. Sometimes I smell Lysol and know there's been a clean freak staying there, one of those people who worries how often the bedspreads are washed and imagines lethal germs crawling all over the bathroom.

They needn't. I'm a good cleaner, thorough, and honest, too. Anything I find after someone has left, from a nickel to a brassiere to a book, I've always turned in to the office. Some of the other maids kid me. They call me "Honest Angie" and say I make things harder for them. But it's always been easier this way, not having to think about it. My minister says God can see all we do, and in God's mind why should a nickel be different from a hundred-dollar bill?

When I clean a room, I shake out the bedspread and check it to see if needs washing—otherwise it goes on a once-a-week wash schedule. I strip the bed and change the sheets, throw away all trash and newspapers and such, replace the wastebasket liners, dust lightly, check the drawers to see if anything was left behind, replace anything that was moved, vacuum, and then I do the bathroom. I swish cleaner into the toilet bowl, tub, and basin, wipe down the entire sink area, clean the mirror, then scrub where I put the cleaner down. When I have time I give the shower curtain a quick wipe, too, to prevent mildew. Right before I leave, I spray our signature potpourri spray into the center of the room then close the door behind me. I want people to walk into the room and just feel that it's clean without even having to think about it.

My friends ask whether I don't get tired of cleaning and not want to do my own home, but I really don't mind. I like the sense of making things better. The pay is decent, I get some benefits, there's no heavy lifting, I don't smell like fried catfish, and it helps a lot with the kids' expenses. I'm teaching my oldest, Kayla, how to clean properly, so that she can keep a nice home, too, but I hope for better things for her, an office job with a good salary. She doesn't say anything, but I know it pains her to have her mother working as a hotel housekeeper, a maid. I just try to show her what it's like to take pride in your work, no matter what you do. My mother worked for years for a lady in Little Rock, who died recently with her two sisters in a helicopter crash in Hawaii, but by then my mother was retired.

When I was growing up, our state motto was "Land of Opportunity," which I always liked. You'd see it on every license plate, like an inspiration, that you could have a better life if you worked hard, that you had a chance. Now it's "The Natural State," which I feel like is just a slogan for tourism, not for the people who actually live here. Working in the hotel industry, though, I guess I should be in favor of all the tourists we can get.

Of course, when people are staying more than one night, the cleaning routine is a little bit different. We don't touch anybody's things, just clean around them. That's how I got into trouble, moving a suitcase. It was one of those duffel things, and there was a crumbled cracker under the corner of it. I lifted it up to vacuum the crumbs then set it back down. They were out for a run, just for an hour, so I had to hurry and get the room cleaned.

Not too long after they came back, my manager, Mr. Kirby, called me down to his office.

"Angie, did you clean 313?" he said.

"Yes, sir," I said. "While they were out."

"Did you see anything lying around?"

I thought for a second. "Like what? I mean, they're unpacked. There's lots of stuff lying around."

"Like a digital camera," he said.

I could see this was bad. "No, sir."

"They say that they had the camera out before they went for a run, and when they came back it was nowhere to be found."

"Mr. Kirby," I said. "You know how honest I am. You know I never take anything, not even the smallest little thing. There must be some mistake."

"I know, Angie," he said, looking at the nameplate on his desk, *Clifton Kirby*, instead of at me, "but these are preferred member guests, and they're raising a stink, and I really just have no choice but to let you go."

I was in shock. I was his best employee and he was firing me for nothing. Then my lip started to twitch and I could tell I was about to either cry or blurt out something I'd regret, so I just said, "I'll return my uniform tomorrow," and hightailed it out of there.

I don't remember driving home. As soon as I got in the door I tore off my uniform and threw it in the washing machine. The kids came home from school, Bobby came home from work, I cooked supper, we ate, I helped the kids with their homework and got their clothes ready for school the next day, then Bobby and I sat down to watch TV before bed and I told him.

"That old bastard," was the first thing he said. "Just shows where being good gets you. Can you remember anything, any way that camera could've gotten misplaced?"

I told him I'd been over and over it in my mind, and I couldn't think of anything. Their mistake, but I was getting blamed for it. I told him I'd go back to the Catfish Cabin tomorrow and see if they had any openings. Some pay was better than no pay at all, and at least I got to bring home free food.

Bobby believes in me, which is why I love him so much still, after three kids and a fair amount of troubles.

"You're the best," he said. "Anybody'd be lucky to have you."

The next morning I took the laundered uniform back to the hotel. Not stopping to talk to Carla, cleaning down the hall, I knocked on Mr. Kirby's door, my face fixed, and stepped inside when he said, "Come." He never says, "Come in," just "Come," as though that one little extra syllable is just too big a time-waster.

"Oh, Angie," he said. "Big mistake. Turns out that couple found the camera inside their duffel bag between the lining and the outside canvas. Must have just slipped in there somehow." He paused. "The job's yours again if you want it. No hard feelings. You've already been officially terminated, so your last pay raise won't be included—company policy—but your benefits will continue as per previously."

What could I say? I made double there what I could get at any restaurant in town. Kayla needed new shoes, Chase wanted to play football this year, and Amber had just discovered the guitar and would want lessons. I took the job back, put on my uniform, and got back to work. No one had even touched my work cart; everything was still in its place, as though I'd never left.

The second room I cleaned (men's aftershave, cigar, shoe polish), when I shook out the bedspread three shiny coins flew into the air, catching the sunlight: two quarters and a nickel. They fell onto the floor, and I stood and looked at them for a full minute before picking them up and putting them in my pocket.

On my break, I went to the vending machine and bought a candy bar. It was sweet, chocolatey, chewy, nutty, and though I searched my soul and examined my conscience, I did not feel the least bit guilty. If God did not understand, I would figure out a way to explain it to Him, when the time came.

Be Careful What You Wish For

One week before my forty-hmmth birthday my husband, Stuart, sat down beside me on the couch, where I was doing the newspaper acrostic, and asked me what I wanted for my birthday. Unlike a lot of husbands, Stuart has never forgotten my birthday in two years of dating and seventeen of marriage, and he always asks if there's something I particularly want. Sometimes there isn't, and he buys me a good but not extravagant piece of jewelry and takes me out to a nice restaurant. Sometimes there is. This was one of those years.

I had thought about how to say it, had waited for him to bring up the question.

"Actually," I said, "I was thinking about having a little work done."

Stuart smiled. "You are a beautiful woman and I love you just the way you are. And I did even before you had your eyes done and your breasts oomphed up."

"Oh, Stuart," I said. "You are the best of husbands. But what I was thinking of, was, maybe, *you* having a little work done."

He frowned, looked down at the couch, and smoothed the nap with his hand. I could hear him thinking that he needed to be fair and hear me out. He relaxed his brow, at least as much as he could with the wrinkles that were permanently there. "Well, OK, what are you thinking about?"

"Stuart," I said, "You are a wonderful and youthful and energetic man. But your face does not necessarily reflect that. What if you had a little

Botox here and there, maybe a little trimming and tightening under the chin, a little eye tuck? Wouldn't you feel better?"

"The point is," he said, "that it would be a present for you. And if that would make you happy, I will do it."

Stuart has almost no fear of physical pain, having been a football player in high school and college. Instead of becoming a coach/history teacher, he got his B.A. and then stayed on for a degree in higher education administration. Afterwards he came back to our hometown to be a high school principal. I knew he'd have a few weeks in the summer with no duties, and I'd taken the liberty of making an appointment with my plastic surgeon for a consultation in May and then the surgery in June.

That night we made love with extra intensity. I don't know what Stuart was thinking—I'm not sure I ever do in those circumstances—but I was picturing a more youthful-looking Stuart, who was also still the man I loved after all these years of marriage, and feeling truly grateful that he would actually be willing to undergo surgery to make me happy. "Happy Birthday," I thought to myself. "Hap-py Bir-ir-irth-Day!"

It was not too hard to arrange to be gone for a couple of weeks in the summer; we usually took one week in Florida and this time we just made it two. We played Summer Doubles in tennis at the Country Club in June (coming in second behind Bitty and Ted Kramer) and booked in at our usual golf and tennis resort in the Panhandle for mid-July. We drove down to Little Rock, Stuart had his surgery and an overnight at the residence attached, and the next day I drove us down to Florida. We had to stop several times to get ice cups at McDonald's to keep his swelling down, but otherwise it went great. For two weeks we relaxed, had room service, sat on the balcony, and Stuart even got in some golf in the second week. I spent time at the pool and worked on my tan. Stuart's a strawberry blond, with fair skin, like Robert Redford, so he doesn't tan much anyway. I had thought of that for coming back from vacation, what people would say.

I have to say, I enjoyed babying him, and he enjoyed the attention.

and pans and dishes. I took heart in the temporary look of the move. He left his award plaques and trophies, the family photos, his big chair.

I know now it was all in my head, that I imagined him wanting to have an affair because he looked better and women were more interested. And even though he always said the two of us were enough, that we didn't need anybody else, I had thought that maybe we'd be one of those couples who have a late baby despite never having been able to conceive before.

Alone in our big bed at night, I try to feel God's love, imagine his all-powerful warmth coursing through me, but I must have some failure of the imagination when it comes to that. Mostly I just think about how foolish I was to want Stuart to have the surgery in the first place, then to go wacko on him when he did what I asked.

I try not to talk about personal stuff at work but when Father Oliphant caught me crying at my desk it was hard not to. We went into his office and he closed the door, as I had seen him do so many times, from the other side, when one of the church members, or sometimes a couple in trouble, showed up to talk to him. His name is Ted Oliphant and the children of the church often call him Father Elephant before they know better, and their parents encourage them in this because they think it's cute. I don't, really, but it did strike me that he is kind of like an elephant in being older and wise. I saw a documentary on elephants that talked about how much they remember, and know, and how they look out for each other and remember who has died.

I told Father Oliphant the whole thing, even the plastic surgery, which I hadn't told anybody about. He listened without being shocked or, what would have been worse, amused, and then asked me what I thought I wanted.

"I want Stuart back, but I don't know if he'll come back."

"If he did come back, do you think things would be different?" I think this was his nice way of asking whether I thought I could change.

"I don't know," I said, miserable with my own weakness. "I think he'd have to believe that they would be, that I wouldn't have this jealousy problem, if he did."

"It's like the Lyle Lovett song," said Father Oliphant, "you know the one, where he talks about who'll forgive you anything and take anything from you and still love you and then says 'God will, but I won't, That's the difference between God and me.'"

I was afraid he was going to go all religious on me then, but he didn't, really. He just said, "Susan, you could start by accepting yourself as you are and see where that takes you."

It's now been two weeks since Stuart moved out, and we have had a couple of inconsequential phone calls, which he keeps deliberately on the light side. He is waiting for me to be able to talk calmly and waiting to figure out what he thinks, I can tell. Yesterday was my birthday, the first time in twenty years without him. He sent a card but didn't call. I went to lunch in Little Rock with my girlfriends, who know about Stuart moving out but don't know about the surgery. We went to a fancy place with cute waiters and flirted shamelessly with ours.

"Shoot," Sharon said. "It's not even the least bit like cheating—he's probably gay anyway."

"Besides," said Charlotte, "it'll do you good, Susan. Stuart just doesn't know what he's missing. You look great, girl!"

I smiled, pretended to have a good time, ate a big piece of "Death by Chocolate" cake for a birthday dessert, and told them what good it had done me so that they could tell themselves afterwards that they'd done the right thing, which in fact they had. I would've done the same for them.

Tonight when I looked in the mirror and noticed my eyelids sagging a bit, I put the thought out of my mind and changed into my nightgown. But first, before I did that, I left my clothes off and stood in front of the full-length mirror, just standing and looking. By pretending I wasn't me but someone else, I saw an all-right-looking forty-three-year-old woman who could be in a lot worse shape, who could be alone instead of with good friends and a good job and a husband who maybe still loved her. I thought maybe I could like this person, if she'd give me a chance.

Compound

I did what I did, and God alone will judge me.

Thomas was gone to town that day to buy supplies, taking the boys with him, so I was alone in the house and in charge of things. Thomas's cousin Jason and his wife, Rachel, had been staying with us, but they were gone for the day, too, applying for jobs.

The boys had been especially noisy lately and I was sort of looking forward to a quiet day at home, digging some weeds, doing some laundry, maybe taking a little time to sit by myself on the porch and drink a cup of tea. It was Friday, so I would write a letter to my mother in prison, as I have done every Friday for the last fifteen years, so she knows I have not forgotten her even if I still have trouble forgiving what she did to Daddy, no matter how mean he got when he was drunk.

But the Lord says we must forgive our enemies, and she is not even my enemy, so I work on that and try to focus on how hard Daddy worked to keep us fed and clothed and housed and how careful Mama was with the household to keep us respectable. I hold a happy memory I have worn smooth as a polished rock of when the four of us, Mama, Daddy, me, and my little sister, Rebecca, went swimming at a creek outside of Fayetteville. We took a big picnic, swam and laughed and played and then rested, and nobody got mad at anybody. It is a perfect memory.

This particular Friday, I was out in the back yard hanging laundry on the line—it was a bright, early spring day—when I heard voices across from the next ridge. We own all this land and it's posted, so somebody was where they shouldn't have been. I went inside for the binoculars and spotted them crossing the old pasture. There was two of them, a man and a woman. They looked old enough to be retired, and they wore jeans and khaki vests with lots of pockets and binoculars around their necks. Birders, I figured. They were talking to each other like they were both really interested in what the other one was saying. The man had a fancy walking stick, and the woman wore a hat over her short white curly hair. They reminded me of nothing more than little baby mice, pink and fresh.

It was a shame. I knew what I had to do. Thomas had given us all strict instructions about intruders. You never knew who you could trust or what kind of disguises the government agents might take on. Ever since we stopped paying taxes, took the boys out of school, and made a formal affiliation with the Brotherhood, we have been expecting the government to come. A person just can't live on his own anymore, following his own beliefs. No, the government and all the Jews and Blacks and other Foreigners have ruined that for normal White Americans, even those that have served their country faithfully, like me and Thomas and Jason have.

You have to kill the baby mice or they will overrun your house. I went back inside for my rifle, came out on the deck, took a breath and exhaled, sighted the man, and squeezed the trigger. I am a good marksman, and he dropped immediately. Almost before the woman knew what happened, I sighted and dropped her, too. People look surprised when they get shot, before the pain hits. I took them out as humanely as possible, then ran down the hill to be sure they weren't suffering any. My steps sounded loud in the leaves, and our dogs Teeter and Griff followed along with me, making more noise. I didn't like leaving the house unprotected, but there was no other choice. I didn't think anyone was with them, but I had to be sure nobody showed up from the other side of the pasture.

By the time I got there, they were both about gone. I knew I had to stay strong. I gave each of them a shot in the head and carried dry leaves over to their bodies for temporary cover. Then I said the Lord's Prayer over them. When I got to the part about "Forgive us our trespasses, as we forgive those who trespass against us," I thought about those words in a way I never had before. These people had literally trespassed against us. They probably were birders, and I was sad that they had decided to come onto our land, but it is posted "no trespassing." I forgave them right there for trespassing against me, though.

Then I went back to the house to wait for Thomas and figure out what to do with the bodies. There was a lot of blood, and you had to think somebody would miss them eventually.

Thomas wasn't angry, not that I'd thought he would be. We told the boys we had some grown-up work to do and sent them to their rooms to play, and the two of us drove the four-wheeler with the trailer attachment down to the bodies. We'd filled the trailer about half-full of sawdust to absorb the blood.

Thomas looked at the bodies then looked at me. "Theresa," he said, "I'm proud of you. I didn't know if you could do it, if it came down to that, but you did good."

I didn't say anything. He didn't expect it.

"Too bad for them," he said. "People ought to know better. They think the world is just an open, free place, think nothing of crossing other people's boundaries. And they've probably raised their children to think the same. Nobody respects property rights anymore." Thomas is redheaded with pale skin and blue eyes and a strong jaw. We met in the army and got engaged three weeks after our first date. We wanted the same things: a close family, a place of our own with a lot of land, and the freedom to follow our own beliefs, meaning a return to America's roots of Christian piety and individual responsibility.

We decided to take them across the pasture, further away from the house, and up to some old caves Thomas had scouted as possible firearms caches. Snakes wouldn't be active yet, so we could get them pretty far back in and use rocks to seal up the mouth. They wouldn't both fit in the trailer, so we took her first then came back for him. Already they were starting to be not like people anymore, more like large stuffed dolls. We'd changed to old clothes we could burn later, and we took their bird book, which had his name, Roland Anderson, in the front, and his wallet and her fanny pack to burn, too. There were enough rocks around to seal up the cave pretty well, and after we'd done that we went back to the place and shoveled the sawdust back in the trailer and spread more dry leaves. We'd burn the soiled sawdust as well.

The whole thing took about two hours, by which time it was dusk. A sweet moist smell rose up out of the pasture, and the setting sun lit the bare tree limbs, just beginning to bud, with a kind of purplish haze. I felt tired but in a good way, and a little sad but not uneasy. Like mice. Nothing else to do.

I almost kept the bird book. I've been wanting to learn more about birds now that we live around so many of them. But finally I had to agree with Thomas that it was dangerous evidence, and we burned it.

The next day we looked in the paper for a story about missing people. We always read the paper out of Harrison because Thomas says it's important to know what the enemy is up to. The story appeared on the third day. A reward was offered. The sheriff was investigating. All we have to say if anyone asks is that we saw and heard nothing. End of story.

No Legacy Is So Rich As Honesty

For as long as I remember recognizing my female family members as Mama and Aunt Sis and Aunt Belle, my mother and her two sisters have been "the three sisters," and their three daughters, including me, have been "the three cousins." Then I grew up and married Jack Musgrove and had three children, known as "the three Musketeers," in a kind of a pun on our last name. My cousins, Sally and Kath, older than me by two years and born only a day apart, don't have kids, Kath because she and her husband, Mike, can't and Sally because she's had two hit-and-run marriages whose only visible byproduct was alimony.

Little Rock is officially a city but is really an overgrown small town where most of the people we know, know each other, and you can predictably see the same people at Christmas pageants, Fourth of July celebrations, and most major weddings and funerals. The Websters, my mother's side of the family, have been here for four generations, and in the state of Arkansas for three more before that. We are not wealthy but we are established. We have a sense of belonging here and of being known for more than one generation. Our mothers became somewhat notorious as seventy-something wild women, liable to wear matching sequined evening gowns, like a trio of back-up singers, to a dull Country Club luncheon, picket a Republican fundraiser dressed in red, white, and blue overalls, or take an elaborate picnic to the cemetery and then spend hours cleaning the graves no one else keeps up.

It was on one of their more adventurous adventures that their exploits came to a sudden end, one that saddened us all deeply but also, incidentally, threw us into confusion. My mother, Sue Anne, is three years younger than Aunt Sis and Aunt Belle. To celebrate my mother's seventieth birthday, the three sisters decided to take a trip to Hawaii. Sally, who is Belle's daughter, had been there on her first honeymoon and had raved about it, and all the sisters had been wanting to go there ever since. It takes a long time to get to Hawaii from Arkansas, so they packed lots of provisions for the journey: lemon squares and peanut butter cookies, tiny bottles of expensive hand creams and under-eye moisturizers, eye pads, inflatable neck rests, and a pashmina for each of them, to keep the chill off. Aunt Sis also had a nice supply of tranquilizers because she hates to fly, which makes what happened to them all the odder.

From what we can tell, now that things have settled down and we have had their funerals and gotten official reports from the authorities and even had one kind phone call from the owner of the helicopter service, who Kath said was probably just calling to keep us from suing her even though they had all had to sign releases, they had splurged on a volcano-viewing helicopter trip, an hour-long sunset-over-the-volcano tour that was supposed to take them closer than you could ever get by car or on foot. I hope it was beautiful. I hope it was magnificent, that the last thing they saw was so breathtaking that they perhaps weren't aware that hot air updrafts from the volcano were making the helicopter dip and dive and then plunge into the mouth of the volcano in a fiery crash that, we're told, would have killed them instantly. Teary and tired after their shared funeral service, we imagined Aunt Sis, always a card, wisecracking from beyond the grave: "I said I wanted to be cremated, but this is ridiculous."

We couldn't believe we'd lost them all at once, and ten or twenty years younger than we'd been preparing for. I'm forty-eight, Sally and Kath are fifty so we're grown-up—more or less as mature as we're going to be and certainly not in need of hands-on mothering, but I'd always imagined my mother helping me with the weddings of my twin girls and spending more time talking as we grew older. Now the three of us were on the front lines. We were suddenly the older females of our family. It felt weird.

Aunt Belle was widowed—Uncle Bobby had died two years ago of cancer, and Aunt Sis and Uncle Bud had been divorced for twenty years. My own father, a quiet man who avoids conflict and is happy if he can smoke his cigar and read his newspaper in peace when he gets home from his job as a corporate loan officer at the bank, has been walking around in a state that I can only describe as permanent surprise, as though he can't believe Mama isn't just going to walk in the door one day and start cleaning house. I think not having a body makes it harder for him, being from an older generation. He calls me at least once a day with a question: "Where does she keep the peanut butter?" or "How often do you change the sheets?" or "Which setting on the dryer is for shirts?" or, once, when he'd probably had one too many glasses of Scotch, "Why did she take such a silly chance, when she knows we need her?"

I've heard that several different women have already asked him out, and I've been afraid he will succumb to one of them. He keeps a beautiful lawn and prides himself on his flower borders and his rose beds, and the house has never for a day appeared less than spick-and-span on the outside, but inside things are starting to get away from him, even after Kath, Sally, and I organized a cleaning brigade to keep the house in proper shape. He doesn't have a knack for domestic order, and he loves to eat but hates to cook. I only hope, if it has to happen, we can nudge him in the direction of someone we like, someone who hasn't leapt on him like a vulture with red lipstick in a pantsuit.

The three of us also decided to clean out Aunt Sis's and Aunt Belle's houses together. We went to Aunt Sis's house first because she was the tidy sister. Aunt Belle was a total packrat, and we knew she would take a while. Aunt Sis had moved into a smaller house after the divorce and had gotten rid of a lot then, so Kath was neither cleaning out her childhood home nor having to deal with the accumulations of a lifetime. When we came in, we saw that Aunt Sis had left the bed made, the laundry done, the dishes clean and put away, everything in such perfect order you might think she had had a premonition, but that was the way she always left things. "I like my place neat as a pin," she used to say, "and with no husband to leave his undershorts on the floor, I can have my way." By the time she and Uncle Bud divorced they seemed less angry at one another than just tired of putting up with each other. He spent more and more time away at the fishing cabin until one day he just didn't come back. She drove his clothes out there one day and that was it.

Her place had a slightly powdery smell to it, as though someone had just bathed. The curtains, feminine and flowery, had begun to accrue slight bits of dust, something Aunt Sis never would have allowed to happen when she was alive.

Kath said, "Is there anything y'all want to keep? Otherwise I'm going to take it all to the Salvation Army. We don't have room for much else at our house."

Kath packed the family photos and her mother's silver for herself, Sally kept two china figurines she'd loved since childhood, and I took a nesting set of colored mixing bowls. There was a single filing cabinet that we figured we should go through; Kath is a CPA and thought she should check on anything financial, although she already knew she would inherit everything according to her mother's will.

Sally and I plopped onto the couch while Kath sat at the desk, glancing through files. We were basically making conversation, remembering childhood birthday parties and trips to the mountains, trying, I think, to keep Aunt Sis alive in our minds. At some point I realized that Kath had gone silent, that papers were no longer being shuffled. I looked over at her. She was staring at a piece of paper, her face perfectly still, her eyes wide and disbelieving.

"Kath?" I said. "Kath?"

She turned. "I don't understand this. This doesn't make sense. I don't understand it."

Sally crossed to the desk and looked over Kath's shoulder. "It's a birth certificate. It's your birth certificate."

Kath said, "It says I was born at 12:14 A.M. and my mother is Anna-Belle Webster Lamont and my father is Robert Thomas Lamont. I don't understand. This is not the birth certificate I have at home. This says Aunt Belle and Uncle Bobby are my parents." She spoke directly to Sally. "This says we're sisters."

Sally said, "I was born at 11:57 P.M. To AnnaBelle Webster Lamont and Robert Thomas Lamont. They always said, 'Kath and Sally, born a day apart.'"

"Our shared birthday parties," said Kath. "So what the hell does this mean?"

"I think it means we're sisters," said Sally.

"Well, obviously!" said Kath, standing up from the desk and bumping her hip. She winced. "I think I need to get out of here."

I suggested we all go back to my house and have a drink. Jack had just gotten home from work when we arrived.

"Crisis," I said. "Major. Kath. Can you get yourself something to eat, and I'll explain later?"

Jack nodded. "Sure. No problem."

I love that about him, his patience and steadiness. He was looking through the day's mail on the counter when I took a bottle of wine and three glasses out to the pool, where Sally and Kath waited.

Kath took one look at the wine and said, "I need a *drink* drink. Bourbon on the rocks."

"You got it," I said, putting down the glasses and bottle and returning to the kitchen. As I headed toward the liquor cabinet, Jack raised his eyebrows.

"Kath," I said. "Bourbon."

"That bad, huh?" he said.

"Beyond."

Back outside, seated in a semicircle, we all looked at each other, still in disbelief, not sure what to say. There would be a storm later, and already little breezes were ruffling the calm of the pool. The wavelets refracted the lights that had come on with dusk, and with the late, lingering green of summer's end overhanging and surrounding us, I felt as though we were in an underwater room, three mermaids contemplating their lives.

"What I don't get," said Sally, "is how we never found out. You'd think it would've come out somehow, that somebody, sometime, would've slipped and told us."

"What about at the hospital?" I said. "The doctor knew. The nurses knew. Probably the obstetrician had known for a while. How on earth did they pull it off?"

Kath sipped at her bourbon. Her bangs were a bit long, falling into her eyes, and she seemed to brood through a curtain of brown hair. It worried me when she got this quiet. Usually she was fast-talking, sometimes foulmouthed—when we were children, she was the last one to stop talking at a slumber party and the first to speak as she awakened. Her husband, Mike, claims that the phrase "Shut up and kiss me" was invented just for her.

"You know," said Kath. "I thought we were nice people, the kind of people who didn't do this kind of thing. We have our personal screw-ups, sure, but we are just not the kind of people this shit happens to. This kind of thing is supposed to be the province of trailer trash, people who show up on afternoon TV talk shows and yell and weep and throw chairs. 'Mothers who steal their daughters' boyfriends' kind of shit. 'Men who sleep with their babysitters.' Well how about 'Mothers who give up one of their twins to their sister'?"

Sally and I didn't say anything. I looked at a bed of impatiens, all leggy and faded, and thought that before long it would be time to pull them and put in pansies. I like flowers, but my kind of gardening is pretty basic. I think now I was probably in avoidance mode. I don't like drama, and this was clearly going to be dramatic. Already was.

"The thing is," she said, getting louder and louder. "The thing is, I don't know who the fuck I am! How the fuck could they do this to me?!"

"Kath," I said. "The neighbors." And regretted it immediately. Why should I care what the neighbors thought when my cousin was having her foundations shaken?

She turned to me, her eyes crazy and dark. "I don't give a flying fuck about the neighbors, Beth. I don't care if the whole goddamn town hears me. For all I know, they all know already. We're probably the only ones who didn't know."

I had made one mistake, and now I made a second. "But we're still all us, Kath. We're still family."

Sally scooted her chair back just a bit, sensing the barrage about to come.

Kath's voice got scary quiet. "No, Beth. You're still you. Cautious. Careful. Good. I, on the other hand, am some kind of bizarre orphan stepchild foundling. My mother is my aunt, my aunt and uncle are my mother and father, one of my cousins is my sister, and my father is some poor bastard with a low sperm count who had the misfortune to get mixed up with my crazy-ass family."

On cue, heat lightning flashed in the southern sky, and a low rumble in the distance reminded me of the storm to come.

"I'm sorry, Kath," I said. "I want things to be OK, and they're not. I'll talk to Daddy tomorrow and try to find out more."

Sally spoke up. "I can't believe we're sisters. Fraternal twins, even. Me born just before midnight, you born just after. All our combined birthday parties. How did they do it? How did they keep up the fiction? I always felt close to y'all, *like* sisters, but what if Kath and I had grown up as real sisters?"

Suddenly I felt that same old exclusion I'd felt as a child, two years younger, always tagging along on Kath and Sally's coattails, feeling more-or-less accepted but not really wanted. They arrived at bras, periods, makeup, boys ahead of me, giggled together over "going all the way" when they got to college, insisted that I drink only Coke at parties so that I could drive them home when they got drunk. I felt bad for thinking about myself at a time like this, but I was starting to cry.

Kath and Sally had stood up and were hugging. Both of them were crying, too.

We were all in shorts and T-shirts, still grubby from our house-cleaning-out work.

"What we need," I said, "is a swim."

Kath and Sally looked up at me as though I was an idiot.

"I mean it. Jump. Last one in is—"

"A rotten leg," said Sally, completing our childhood mishearing of the cliché.

So we jumped. Held hands, ran the few steps, and jumped in a great splash of water and bubbles and our own bodies—related, connected, us.

Coming up, we clasped our hands around each others' shoulders in a huddle and just breathed. I could smell Sally's flowery perfume, Kath's herbal shampoo. Water dripped from our hair back into the pool, and our arms around one another felt animal, primitive, tribal.

"Shit," said Kath. "Shit shit shit shit shit."

Sally laughed.

Kath laughed.

Then they locked eyes, looked at me, and dunked me. I came up spluttering, and they laughed some more.

Eventually we dried off, ordered a pizza, drank some wine, and got sleepy. I put Kath to bed in the guest room and called Mike and told him that it had been upsetting cleaning out Aunt Sis's house, and that Kath would be sleeping at my house for the night. His quizzical response told me he suspected that wasn't the whole story, but all he said was that he'd come by in the morning and pick her up.

In bed, finally, I did tell Jack the whole story. His hazel eyes searched mine as they always did when he was worried about me.

"You OK?"

"Yeah. Kath's a little volatile right now, and a little drunk, too, but I think we're all basically OK."

"Well, really, she should be able to get past this. Everybody did it with the best intentions, and she grew up loved and protected by lots of people."

"It's just that she doesn't really see it that way. She's the one who got given away, the one whose life was altered without her choice, so that in a sense she was robbed of her real parents. You know she never got along very well with Uncle Bud."

"Everything'll look better in the morning, I promise," said Jack, turning out his bedside light. I read a page in my book and realized nothing was computing, so I turned mine out, too.

The next day was a Saturday, and I called my father and asked if I could come over.

He was working on the rose bushes when I arrived, wearing his leather gloves, fertilizing and mulching and watering his various old-fashioned varieties. I don't know much about them, but he can recite their names like old friends: Alexandre Girault, Cecile Brunner, and Old Blush, to name a few he has managed to teach me.

There was a hint of fall in the air and we got cups of coffee and sat outside.

"Daddy," I began, "we were clearing out Aunt Sis's place yesterday when Kath found something in her files."

He looked across at the roses, as though still thinking about them. "Hmmm?"

"Something that didn't make sense."

His eyes, hooded like a hawk's, swiveled toward me, sharp and piercing.

I told him about the birth certificate, how it seemed that Kath and Sally were both Aunt Belle and Uncle Bobby's children, twin sisters, and how Aunt Sis had produced a different birth certificate for Kath when she was a teenager going to get her Social Security card so she could get a summer job, and how we didn't understand, any of us, and how Kath was a mess and was still, in fact, asleep in my guest bedroom.

"Well," he said, "what do you want to know?"

I almost leaped up out of my seat but instead just leaned forward, my knees touching his. "What we want to know, Daddy, is why. Why on earth would anybody do such a thing, and why didn't anybody stop them?"

He took a deep breath, as though preparing to testify in court. I half expected him to hold up his right hand and place his left on the Bible. "Sis couldn't have children. Belle found out she was going to have twins and decided it was God's way of taking care of the both of them. It took some work, talking Sis into it, then talking Bobby into it, and finally Bud. I think it was hardest on Bobby, but you know he never went against what Belle wanted, if she really wanted it."

"And you and Mama?"

"You know those women, Bethie. Nobody could say no to them once they made up their minds. Nobody dared. And your mother was their baby sister. I had my doubts, but I was new to the family and didn't know how much I could, or should, say."

"And Kath's fake birth certificate?"

"They filed the adoption papers immediately. Sis must've gotten rid of those if you didn't find them. Then she went to the courthouse and just paid one of those clerks a hundred dollars for a new birth certificate. People used to do that kind of thing more, sometimes people from the country who'd never had their birth recorded but for some reason or another needed a birth certificate for Social Security or whatever, they'd just pay off a clerk and get one. Or a woman who'd had a baby out of wedlock and turned it over to relatives. It's not like now, when being an unwed mother is hardly even cause for shame."

We sat for a minute, several minutes I guess, while I took the news in. The chimes Mama had given Daddy for his birthday moved in the breeze, low and mellow sounding. Daddy coughed, and I realized his eyes were watering.

"I'm sorry, Daddy," I said. "I'm sorry to dredge it up, and I'm sorry about Mama, and I'm sorry you're lonely."

He smiled. "Lonely is not so bad. But these women. Sue Anne's been gone five weeks and one of them asked me at church last week when I was going to stop wearing my wedding ring. Can you believe that?"

I shook my head. "You just keep on wearing it. I miss her, too." I was glad to hear him say that, of course, even though I knew he might want to remarry someday. I just didn't want it to be too soon.

"There's one more thing I need to ask," I said. "Do people know?"

He looked across the yard at his neighbor, Mr. Schiller, washing his car, and waved back to Mr. Schiller's wave. "Well, they did. I don't know how much people think about it, they have their own troubles, you know, but at the time some people must have known. They didn't explain it to anyone, of course, but the information was out there, from the hospital if nowhere else. They decided ahead of time that Belle would take the first one and Sis the second, and they each took a baby home from the hospital." He was looking up into the sky now, back in memory. "Belle nursed Sally and Sis fed Kath on the bottle, except when they were together and then Belle would sometimes nurse Kath, too. Sis and Bud lived in Conway and when they came home with a baby, people just assumed an adoption and didn't ask too many questions. Then they moved to Little Rock a few years later, by which time the gossip, if there was any, would've died down."

He stopped talking. He looked tired around his eyes, like he hadn't been sleeping well, and I felt guilty for adding this additional burden. But he was the only one left to ask. Already since my mother died I had wanted to ask her a hundred questions, from when, exactly, to plant jonquil bulbs to Great-Aunt Sally's apple butter recipe to when her menopause started, but every single question just turned back on itself, a reminder that all the answers had died with her. I wished then that Aunt

Sis and Aunt Belle's secret had died with them as well. What good could it do Kath now, what I had to tell her?

I sat in Kath's kitchen, sunlight pouring through the stained-glass window she and Mike had bought from a church that had been deconsecrated and was to be torn down. I had always loved that kitchen, warm, homey, uncluttered, nearly Shaker in its clean wood surfaces with everything you needed but nothing extra. She and Mike had hoped for children but had been happy together without them.

She listened while I told her everything my father had said. Her long fingers curled around the mug she held, tightening as I drew to my conclusion.

"So that's it. That's what I found out," I said, watching her.

"You know, Beth, I'm just so pissed off at them all. That they just did it, so highhanded and presumptuous. No wonder I never got along with Bud, no wonder we fought so much. At least Mama was in fact my aunt, but Bud wasn't even related."

"It must have been kind of hard for him," I ventured.

"Yeah, I guess. It's just, if we hadn't fought so much, maybe I wouldn't have spent so much time rebelling. Maybe I'd be a different person now, a better person. I just hate the secrecy of it, the deception. I feel like I need to do something but I don't know what."

The next thing I knew Sally called me first thing in the morning and said, "Have you read the morning paper yet? Look on page B16."

I opened the paper. There, big as Dallas, was an ad, taking up the top corner of the page:

"To whom it may concern: I, Katherine Leigh Meriwether, married to Michael Thomas Meriwether, though secretly adopted and raised by Caroline 'Sis' Leigh Webster Carter (deceased) and Charles 'Bud' Ralph Carter, am the actual biological daughter of AnnaBelle Webster Lamont (deceased) and Robert Thomas Lamont (deceased) and the twin sister of

Sarah Webster Lamont. 'No legacy is so rich as honesty.'"

"Oh, Lord, Sally," I said. "Do you think this'll get it out of her system?"

"I hope so," said Sally. "Maybe nobody will notice. There's a piece on the facing page about a baby alligator that showed up in a Florida mall at a Toys R Us store, and see that big picture with the alligator and a Tickle Me Elmo in its mouth? Maybe nobody'll look at her ad, they'll just see the alligator."

"Yeah, maybe."

As part of her honesty campaign, Kath had decided that she had to talk to Uncle Bud. He had come to the funeral, before we knew anything of course, but had slipped away before anyone had the chance to talk to him, and the two of them didn't talk much anyway.

Uncle Bud was still living in his fishing camp, which he had insulated somewhat for year-round use. Bud, unfortunately, is bad to drink, so Kath went out to catch him at his best time, between 10:00 A.M. and noon, when the first drink of the day had kicked in but he was still clear-headed, and before he took the boat out for his daily fishing and beer drinking.

Kath told Bud that she knew about the adoption, that she and Sally were twin sisters.

"Well," he said, "if you know, what do you need me for?"

Kath said that the whole time they were talking he was tying a lure, his fingers mysteriously agile and steady despite the years of drinking. He rarely looked up at her.

"I want to know from you," she said. "What you thought."

"I loved her," he said. "I wanted what would make her happy. And it did. You did."

"But why not tell me?" Kath demanded, not softened by his sweet words.

"It's a long time ago, sweetheart. Water under the bridge."

"Not for me, it isn't. It's brand-new news. How'm I supposed to just move on?"

"You will. I did."

Kath said she was ready to leave then but decided to go ahead and press on to the question she really wanted to ask. "Why were you so hard on me growing up?"

Kath said he looked at her then, his washed-out blue eyes steady on her face, and took a long drink from his beer. "I was hard on you because I felt like Belle and Bobby were always watching me, after the sacrifice they'd made for Sis. I figured they thought I wasn't good enough for her, which I wasn't, so I tried to act like what I thought a father should. I'm sorry. I tried."

Kath said she cried a little then. "I wish we hadn't fought so much," she told him.

"Me, too," said Bud.

It wasn't exactly a come-to-Jesus moment, but it settled Kath down some.

The next day she came over for lunch, and as we ate our chicken-salad sandwiches, she told me about their conversation. Then she said, "Beth, we're thinking about adopting. I know we're too old and it's crazy and I should wait until the dust settles, but somehow it feels right, like I'd know more about how the child would feel, as a result of all this, and could be a good mother to her." She filled her glass of iced tea so it caught the light, and the ice squares glinted in the bourbon-colored liquid.

"Big step," I said, determined not to walk into another conflict with her.

"It would be," she admitted and sipped at her tea. "But I just want something good to come out of all this, something concrete—more than just some crazy family story, you know?"

"Yeah," I said. "I know."

And that's where we stand now. It remains to be seen whether the adoption plans will go through. If they do, I'm sure Kath will indeed be a good mother. She has more or less absorbed this new information about herself and even talks to Uncle Bud pretty regularly now. But she still rolls her eyes and mock-sighs whenever Sally calls her "Sis."

If Kath had been telling this story, it would've had a lot more exclamation points. If Sally had told it, she would have recorded what everyone was wearing. But I am the one who remembers, who writes down and recalls our crazy family stories. After all, it is *our* crazy family, and it is what we have.

I think, sometimes, that we're a lot like fireflies on a summer evening, all of us flashing like mad at each other in our brief season of life. So easy to get the signals crossed. Such need, as dark falls, to get it right.

1957

When I first learned that the face of the angry, hate-filled woman in the photograph of crowds trying to prevent African-American students from attending Central High School in Little Rock, Arkansas, in September of 1957 was my mother, I ran to the bathroom and vomited up the meatloaf and mashed potatoes and corn she had cooked and served our family for dinner that night.

It was 1972 and I was thirteen years old and being bused to Carver Junior High, a long, low building made of bricks the color of an old scab, surrounded by a chain-link fence with concertina wire at the top, like a prison, and squeezed in between the interstate and a perpetual-care cemetery dotted with faded plastic bouquets.

I was reading my history homework assignment on the 1957 desegregation crisis at Central when I looked at the photo and felt a strange sense of recognition. I walked out into the hallway to look at my parents' wedding photo that same year, then back across the green shag carpeting to my textbook, and then I ran down the hall to the bathroom.

Mom and Dad were watching TV and my brother, Dell, was in his room. After I threw up, I went down the stairs, out the back door through the kitchen, across the back yard, and slipped through the large wooden doors into the old garage, where I kept my cigarettes and matches in an old coffee can half-full of nails. Ever since my father had gotten emphysema, he didn't do yard work anymore, and my mother relied on random yard men who knocked on the front door during the summer. Every once in a while she'd bribe me or Dell to rake leaves or trim hedges, but our yard had a perpetually scraggly look. Some of our neighbors made remarks, but we weren't the kind of family to care about that sort of thing.

I took a seat in the old white curved-metal chair and lit up. A row of windows ran across the top of the wall above the doors, and I could see a network of branches, leaves, and deep-blue dusky sky through the cobwebs and dust collected there. I had forgotten until now, but I used to like to think about space, the universe, infinity, back then. It made me feel small and insignificant and large and important at the same time, small because I was such a speck compared to infinity, large because my mind could contemplate such vastness, as though the universe existed inside my head, in all its mystery and complexity. Back then, though, I probably just thought to myself, "Space is cool."

I was a little shaky that night. Discovering that your mother is a racist is not exactly a happy moment. If I had been pressed, I probably would have said that yes, my parents thought black people weren't as good as the rest of us, but I never thought my mother was the kind of racist who would go to the trouble to get herself down to Central High and stand on the street and yell obscenities at a bunch of high school kids—kids just a little older than me—to keep them from going to school with white kids.

I hated her then. Hated her with the pure, righteous, one hundred percent certainty of adolescence. I was judge, jury, and executioner. But I never spoke of it. I just decided she was a hypocrite, doing what she had done and still going to church twice a week as though she were a good person. For the next four years—ignoring the meals she cooked, the laundry and housecleaning she did, the demands a sick husband made on her—I compiled a mental dossier of her failings until, the minute I could get out of the house, I did. I went to the university on a scholarship for pre-nursing students and then on to nursing school, until I got a job at St. Vincent's, where I have worked for the last twenty-four years in the cardiac unit.

In my freshman year, my dad died of the emphysema. At the same time my friends were taking up smoking, I quit. I got a little fat and stayed that way, but it doesn't hurt a nurse to have an extra bit of heft. People trust a plump nurse.

My dad was the strong, silent type, and then he got sick and became the weak, silent type. After he died, Mom got scraggly, like the yard. The year before, Dell had somehow gotten into the Rhode Island School of Design and, though he found ways to pay for it, he didn't have any extra to come home on. We'd thought he would go to the liberal arts college down the road, but a friend of his had a bad experience there and he changed his mind. I tended to stay in Fayetteville unless I absolutely couldn't figure out anything else to do. One Thanksgiving I claimed I'd been invited to a friend's house, and instead I found an open 7–11 and bought Vienna sausages, crackers, and beer for my holiday feast. I tried to be jaunty about it, but it was depressing, and after that I decided I was better off at home, despite my mother's religiosity and packrat habits that made my old room hard to maneuver in.

Dell surprised me by moving home after a couple of years in New York, where he'd gone once he'd finished at RISD. Said he missed a southern accent. I think maybe he had a bad love affair, but he doesn't talk much about that stuff, even now. I think I knew he was gay even when we were kids. I knew he was different from other boys, anyway. He lives with a black guy named Arthur, a lawyer, and works as an art therapist at the VA. He has a show in New York every five years or so, and his work sells. You might think he'd never see our mother, but he goes over there every Sunday afternoon like clockwork, without Arthur of course, and does little chores around the house, changing a light bulb here or hammering a nail there. Dell's and Arthur's lives might as well exist in a parallel Little Rock universe, occupying the same space as my mother's but in a different dimension.

Dell's given name is Darnell Lee, after our grandfather. From age four on, however, he insisted on being called Dell, which is what I've always known him as. Sometimes people mishear and think his name is Dale.

He corrects them the same way every time: "Not Dale, Dell. Rhymes with Hell."

This year is the fiftieth anniversary of the 1957 crisis, and I saw in the paper the other day that there were a lot of activities planned to mark it, some at Central, some at the Clinton Museum, and a rally against present-day racism, down at the Capitol.

I hadn't thought about that photo in a long time. I guess I'd more or less forgotten about it, repressed it, some people would say. On impulse, I picked up the phone and called my mother. It was Saturday morning, and unless she's gone to the grocery store for something she needs on Sunday, she's usually home. I don't know what she does. Not much. Television, knitting, inspirational reading.

She picked up. "Hello?" Sounding like her voice hadn't been used yet.

"Mom, it's me. I want to ask you something."

"Yeah? OK. What'd you forget?"

"1957. Central High. Were you there? Is that you in the pictures?"

"1957," she said, emphasizing the *fifty*. "Cissy, that was fifty years ago." I waited.

"But yes, I was there. They were trying to make white children go to school with colored children, and I didn't think that was right. Isn't that what they like to call exercising your freedom of speech?"

"Mom, there are pictures of you. In history books. Yelling at those kids."

"Are there?" she said. "Never saw it. Those civil rights photographers, I guess. Making us look bad."

"It was bad, Mom. Do you still not see that?"

"Cissy, what I see is society breaking down. The Bible tells us that Ham sinned and was condemned to blackness, and so God is telling us that the black race is inferior."

"Mom," I said, getting angry, starting not to care what I said. "What about Arthur? Dell's friend. You know about him, whether you admit it or not." I had moved out onto my little balcony and was watching a squirrel twitch his tail in sharp, flicking motions at another squirrel infringing on his territory. Or maybe at me. What do I know about squirrels?

"That . . . nigger?" she said, her voice rising, too. "That *queer* nigger? I don't know what he's done to Dell, brainwashed him I guess. The Bible says men aren't to lay down with men, which I tell Dell every Sunday when he comes over—"

My brother is a saint, I thought.

"—because Dell isn't one of those, you know, he's just too nice to kick this pervert out."

"Oh, God, Mom."

"I'll thank you not to take the name of our Lord in vain," she said.

"God damn it, Mom!" I said, and hung up. I wanted a cigarette so bad I could taste it.

This was not the end, of course. It is never the end with family.

I called her back that afternoon to apologize for hanging up on her.

I said I was sorry. She said: "I'm seventy-five years old, a poor widow woman with a bad back, piles like bunches of grapes, and an ungrateful daughter who blasphemes. Tell me Cissy, what do I have, if I don't have God?"

I said I didn't know, I was really sorry. She said: "When are you going to find a nice man and settle down? Who's going to take care of you when I'm gone? Do you want to be old and alone, like me? Is that what you want?"

"Just haven't found the right man, Mom. You know how hard it is to meet people, the hours I work." What goes unspoken is that I've been Dr. John Wilson's mistress for the last twenty years; I've never known what she knew or didn't, or, for that matter, what John's wife knows or doesn't. But what neither of them knows is that I have no intention of marrying him or anyone else, even if he should become available. I like my life and my apartment tidy, I like to wake up in the morning with my own thoughts, I like to cook and eat what I want when I want. This suits me, suits John, and may even suit Gretchen Wilson. It does not, however, suit my mother.

"You could meet some nice men at church, if you would go."

"Tell you what, Mom. I'll go to church with you tomorrow if you'll come to the 50th anniversary of the Central High desegregation with me."

"Well," she said. "I won't like it, but I'll do it."

"Same here," I said. "See you tomorrow."

The next morning I went to church, where I didn't fall in love with Jesus or any other man.

On Tuesday afternoon I picked up my mother and drove her to Central High. The auditorium was packed, so we took a seat near the back.

First the mayor spoke, then one of the original students who had tried to register for school that day in 1957, and then lo and behold Arthur came up to speak. Looking toward the front for Dell, I thought I recognized the back of his head.

Instead of Martin Luther King or Jesse Jackson style, Arthur was quiet, plain-spoken but powerful. No wonder he is successful in court. He had that audience in the palm of his hand, and I was so caught up in what he was saying I forgot to even look at my mother until I heard a loud, raspy inhalation in my left ear. She was snoring. In the middle of the speech. I was humiliated, then pissed. The woman on the other side of my mother looked towards me, and my face was halfway on its way to a "I'm so sorry, this is hideously embarrassing, can't take her anywhere" grimace, when I looked at *her* face, a kind face with brown eyes framed by brown hair. Her expression was gentle and said, "We've all been there before," as she looked at my mother the way you might look at a small child.

And then I saw what she saw: a tired older woman with a funny gray cowlick, slightly crooked lipstick, and an unfashionable sweater with a small gravy stain on the placket. My heart lurched open, and I knew I wouldn't be able to close it again.

She slept on, snoring, until the end of Arthur's speech and the applause that surged up in response. I felt her perk up next to me and saw her open her eyes alertly. She patted my arm to get my attention and whispered loudly into my ear, "That wasn't as bad as I thought it would be."

We drove home mostly in silence. I was thinking about a couple of black nurses I know, and how I've never really tried to connect with them as people, even though I am always friendly. I had some errands to run, so I just dropped my mother at the curb. She got out, shut the door, then rolled her wrist in a circle to signal me to open the window. When it was all the way down, she put both hands on the frame, her arthritic knuckles bulging, and said, "Cissy, I know about your doctor. Just be sure he treats you right, at least."

"Yes, ma'am," I said. I don't think she wanted any other reply.

She walked toward the house and up the flaking concrete steps to the wooden porch, using the metal railing to steady herself.

When she reached the top, she turned back and stood there for a second, raising her arm in a gesture that might have been a wave, or might have been a dismissal, or maybe was just shielding her eyes from the late afternoon sun, strong now on the west-facing house.

I waved back, just in case, and drove away.

Arkansas Blacks

We were born on an apple farm in 1929, one of us in January, one in December. Almost-twins, they called us, we looked so much alike, and we were never out of the other's sight.

Celia and Delia, even named like twins. Celia Amelia and Delia Aurelia. Our mother believed the doubly doubled rhyming names would protect us, like a charm.

She was not gentle or soft, our mother, but fierce in her love. Her hands were calloused and she scrubbed us hard in the metal tub on Saturday nights, but the water was always warm, the soap scented of roses by her own hand. She meant for us to survive and fed us well.

FIRE

Our mother was in the yard hanging laundry on the line when the fire took hold of the house. She looked around, couldn't find us outdoors, then ran inside screaming "My babies, my babies" and searched for us until she succumbed to the smoke. Hearing a commotion, we came up from the creek, where we'd wandered off to dip our bare feet in the cool flowing water and stuff ourselves with berries. We came around the corner of the house, our mouths purpled with berry juice, and in our father's excited state—he had seen the smoke and come in from the orchards—we must have looked horrific, like ghouls. He screamed. Then he shouted at us: "Where have you been? You've killed your mother!" We believed him. He himself looked like a spaceman, garbed in protective gear and mask for spraying the trees, which were under attack from worms. The Arkansas Blacks, with their characteristic shiny, dark peels, were hit hard by the worms. Like everyone else, we had Ben Davis trees too, but they were not much good for just eating.

That was the first time we died.

Afterwards, he didn't do what some men do, left alone in a house with girl children. He just stopped loving us. He was a good-hearted man, but he lost heart, and he lost the way back to loving us. It was wrong that she died. She was a good mother. We didn't mean for her to die. We just loved berries, the cool water, the idyll of our shared escape.

He repaired the house from the fire damage, not as bad as you would think. Less than a year later he brought home a new wife. Young, skittish, she smiled too often and burned pies. We hated and tormented her, putting salt in the sugar bowl, frogs and lizards and even a young rat snake into drawers she would open and then leap back from, wailing. We hid behind doors and jumped out yelling "boo!" We nearly drove her crazy. We did drive her away.

After she left we took over the housekeeping ourselves, two miniature women in a full-size kitchen. From the time we could walk and hold things without dropping them we had learned to feed the chickens, slop the hog, cook simple food, bake, clean, and wash. We didn't sew our own clothes until high school, so the ladies of the Methodist church brought us their daughters' hand-me-downs. We didn't much care what we wore. Perhaps out of spite, perhaps fear, our father rarely let us go anywhere. We reasoned that to fear losing someone you must love them. He must have loved us. After supper, the meager set of dishes washed and dried and put away in the cupboard, we would sit, the three of us, in the parlor, Father smoking cigarette after cigarette he rolled himself, with careful deliberation, and rocking in his faded old chair. We did not speak. In winter it was dark early and the shadows played in the corners of the room. In summer the light lasted until bedtime, and we often spent long minutes studying the slant of light through our front windows. Beyond his cigarettes, a permanent smell of charred wood permeated our days, invisible, nearly unnoticeable, worse when it rained. What with the worms, then the spraying, then having to wash the spray from the apples once they were picked, prices went up and apples sold less. The farm did badly.

Every November we bake a special pie with Arkansas Blacks and bury it in the ground on Mother's birthday.

THE TOWN ON THE LAKE

We married two brothers so we wouldn't have to be apart, town boys so we could move off the farm. We didn't really care which one we married, so we let them choose. They wanted hard workers, good cooks, patient wives, so our lack of clothes, our simple hair, our quiet, unflirtatious ways did not bother them, perhaps even seemed proof of our solidity. For annual events like a Rotary Club dinner they took pleasure in dressing us up in matching frocks from Rothman's. "New dresses for miladies," they liked to say. "At *least* once a year." It became a kind of joke, one we didn't really get.

As we grew older our father had told us, "Be sure to wash your crotch, girls." We had to figure it out ourselves. We knew what the crotch of a tree was. Finally we saw that if you imagined a tree as a girl standing on her hands, the crotch would be between the legs at the place we called, to ourselves, the opening. We never knew any other words for it until we got married. We never repeated the words we heard.

Once, the doctor examined our openings to see whether he could figure out why neither of us had children. He called them our lady parts. "Your lady parts are fine, girls," he said, not meeting our eyes. "Sometimes it's just God's will."

We didn't mind. We knew something about the hardships of motherhood. Our husbands minded a little because they wanted proof of their manhood, but really they were boys themselves and liked our mothering.

The boys heard that business opportunities were better in the town on the lake and moved us there. They were salesmen, and it was a town for selling, a resort where everything from art and antiques to flesh and whiskey was for sale by somebody, somewhere.

When we bought our annual dresses we always went to the same dress shop where an Irish woman named Maggie Mae waited on us. Each time we came in Maggie Mae would say, "And how are the Irish twins today?" The first time we ever went in, she, like many others, took us for twin sisters, and when we explained that we were born eleven months apart, she told us that children born so in Ireland are called Irish twins. She was a kind woman with a good heart who worked hard to support her large family. She was said to be a wonderful cook whose larder was never empty and from whose table no one ever left hungry. We wanted to know her better but we were shy. We had the distinction of being her only Irish twins, and we liked that.

We didn't know we were good at dancing until the dance studio came to town. The studio offered free lessons to bring in customers and it turned out we were naturals.

The studio had shellacked floors and smelled of wood and lemon oil and perfume and aftershave and clean clothes. The instructor took turns dancing with us and called us his star pupils. Two women in the class, girlfriends of small-time crooks, took a dislike to us. They were pretty and looked like women in magazines and expected to be treated well, or at least noticed first, by men. We should've realized there'd be trouble, but no one had ever envied us before, so we did not see it. The night of our recital we were to do a dance number on a floating pier on the lake in front of the big hotel. The cropped green lawn sloped down gently to the lake and guests gathered there in the evenings to drink and listen to music in the lingering light of summer nights. We were treated to a glass of champagne before we began and it made us giggly and unaware. Our husbands were to show up later in time to watch the dancing.

"Celia, Delia!" the women called to us. "Let's go stand on the pier and be sure we have our sea legs."

We followed, walking carefully if tipsily across the small walkway that led to the pier. The women did a couple of turns. "Yep! Just fine!"

"Oh, look!" one of them said. "Fish! Look, girls!"

Obediently, we stood at the edge and looked down into the water, smelling the rich lake smell and straining our eyes for fish. It must have been easy to push us in, just a tap on the back of each of our already unbalanced bodies. By the time we stood up in the waist-deep water they were gone. Our hair and costumes were ruined.

We did not cry because we don't. But we were mad as two wet cats, and we made a plan. We knew that the walkway was to be pulled away when the dance began, to increase the impression of dancing on water. Two ropes tied to water oaks would hold the pier in place. We found the ropes, untied them, and left them loosely looped around the trees then hid down the lake a bit.

We heard them talking to the instructor in their sharp, loud, artificial voices. "They said they didn't feel good and were going home. Pity."

The dancers walked onto the pier, and the walkway was pulled up. The band began to play a lively tune, and the dancers took their places to do the Charleston, our opening number. Slowly, the pier moved out into the lake. The hotel guests admired the effect, thinking it was intended. One of the women shrieked a bit. A mist was moving in, and it was hard to see them.

We didn't stay for the ending but slipped off home, by good luck not meeting our husbands on the way. We imagined the dancers floating off into the lake, perhaps to be rescued, damp and shivering, by an early morning fisherman. We imagined them floating forever. In real life, however, the next day comes.

Over bacon and eggs the next morning we heard from our husbands that boats were mobilized, the dancers transferred, the pier towed back. The headline in the paper read, "Damp Dancers Escape Drowning After Floating Dock Debacle." We explained to the boys that we had been overcome by nervous stomachs and slipped back home, fearful of meeting them and being talked into coming back. They took us at our word. Other people must have wondered why we had disappeared home when we loved dancing so much, but we never told our side of the story. There was the occasional hint dropped asking where we'd been, but we simply smiled mysteriously and eventually the excitement ebbed. We did not go back to class but kept dancing at home, sometimes forgetting to make the beds, fix supper, even sleep.

Our husbands grew worried, then petulant, then firm. They threatened, cajoled, insisted, put their feet down, but we could not stop dancing, and we could not explain why.

Eventually, we were sent to Benton. For five years we danced all day, every day. Not only with each other, but with each other when there was no dance scheduled and none of the other patients wished to dance. Finally, we danced ourselves out. We agreed to play checkers in the day room, to style our hair, learn weaving, gossip. That was the second time we died.

We were let go, back to our husbands, who seemed remarkably unchanged and had kept one another company in our absence by beginning a bootlegging operation. We were happy to help them. It was not so different from canning.

About that time we joined the Weekly Pie Club, to learn to do something besides dance. Of course, we had learned to bake apple pies growing up on the farm, but in the Weekly Pie Club all of the members baked the same pie, but a new kind of pie, each week, and then we each sampled one another's pies and decided which was best and discussed why. This grew tiresome at times, but in a small town it is more trouble to quit a group than to simply keep going, and we belong to the Weekly Pie Club still, though we have long since run out of new kinds of pie to bake. We have been through many kinds of pie—you can imagine them yourself so there is no use listing them—and our husbands are the happy recipients of half a pie each a week.

We prefer cake, but there is no Weekly Cake Club in our town and we are not the kind to start one. Cakes, for instance, are easier to cut in half than pies, which especially if they are fruit tend to divide sloppily. Although, as our husbands are wont to say, "It doesn't matter how it looks! It's going to get mixed up in my stomach anyway!"

During the time our husbands were making and selling whiskey something happened that we are still mulling over and may still be to the end of our days. It has little to do with whiskey, though. That's just how we measure time.

Our husbands did not take a drop themselves, and they were known for a good product at a fair price. The sheriff got his cut, and it was only when the federal boys came around that there would ever be any trouble. Prohibition was long gone but blue laws forbade alcohol sales on Sunday, along with such things as the sale of playing cards, sewing supplies, and garden tools. Our boys did well on the weekends and in the evenings, when stores closed. The town was not so much lawless as accommodating. A respectable cathouse operated at one end of its wide, curving main street, a big two-story Victorian where the girls were kept healthy and the men anonymous. The county sheriff and the town police were peace officers. They were not given to strict enforcement of the law but rather to maintaining an absence of violence and disruption.

Shows came to the big hotel in those days, great productions with sequins and greasepaint, boas and bow ties. We loved it all, and because the boys supplied the management with their finest backdoor hooch, we got in free. One night an illusionist, who went by the name of Sandor, was performing. Most such acts had big names, with "Magnificent" or "Grand" or "Astonishing" attached, but Sandor was just Sandor. Sandor the Quiet. Sandor the Subtle. Sandor the Sneaky, Slippery, Surreptitious. Sandor the Illusionist.

Magicians love twins, and he picked us, the almost-twins, the Irish twins, out of the audience, a not-full house that night, immediately.

"Ladies, tell me," he smiled confidentially. "What is your fondest wish?"

We answered together without hesitation: "To see our mother again." We had often spoken of this with each other, our hope, even though we did not exactly believe in Heaven, that if we did get to see her in the Afterlife we would finally have the chance to apologize.

Sandor became serious. "When did you last see your mother?"

"When we were seven and eight."

"And what was your mother's name?

"Iris."

"Ladies, your wish is about to come true. In a moment I will ask you to step inside the magic cabinet. I will close the doors, which"—he nimbly stepped into one side of the cabinet, had us close the door, then opened it with a flourish—"you can see open from within, so you cannot be trapped." He then stepped out and we looked in. The cabinet, an old wardrobe, was painted a deep blue all over, with yellow stars inside and white swirls without.

Sandor turned toward the audience. "I will now transport these beautiful ladies to the meeting ground of the living and the dead, the parenthetical space between present and past, the Interland. When I open the cabinet, they will have disappeared!"

We never thought to ask about getting back, so eager were we to see our mother. We stepped into the two sides of the cabinet, and he closed the doors. A whirring arose, a feeling of vertigo, and then nothing.

MOTHER

We awoke on our backs, lying on soft grass, and opened our eyes to apple blossoms and blue sky. A faint scent of rose. A mockingbird chirping and trilling a long song, intended for other mockingbirds. For we all have our song to sing, and not all songs are for everyone.

We walked up to the house, where Mother and Father were just sitting down to dinner.

"Wash your hands, girls," said our mother. "Celia, Delia, you must come when I call so I don't worry."

"Listen to your mother," said our father and gave us each a piece of hard candy for later.

Can you smell an absence? There was no smoke, not even a tendril of scent lingering in a floorboard or chair joint. That night, lying in our twin beds with fresh sheets, we talked. How could we ask her forgiveness for something that had not yet happened? How could we tell her how much we missed her, when she did not yet know?

We would have to live it again.

The next day we walked down to the creek with heavy hearts and ate berries that tasted of ash and waited for the fire to begin.

When we saw the flames, we ran to the house. She was on the porch screaming for us, opening the door, going inside, and our father was running from the orchard, and we were too late.

That night we lay down on blankets by the creek to sleep, a little way off from our father, whom we had never heard sob before, and who frightened us in his loss.

A wind came up, and then a dog began to bark on the far side of the creek, which seemed suddenly wider. The dog's insistent bark would not stop, and we clung to each other. It began to rain, big fat drops spaced widely apart in the dirt and then more and more densely until it seemed a wall of rain was upon us. In the distance our house smoldered. The dog continued to bark.

We could hear the creek rushing past and one of us cried, "Look!"

Coming down between its banks was a huge snake, riding the currents, twisting and bucking the waves, its head above water, its tongue a flicker of cold flame. We stood in the rain and watched it pass, and the dog we had never seen but only heard fell silent.

We felt our father standing nearby, a heavy presence, and without a word he shepherded us to the barn, where we passed the rest of the night.

In the morning we were damp and smelled of hay, and we walked out of the barn into bright daylight. Sleepy, it took us a moment to remember what had happened. Then to wonder if we had dreamed it. The house stood, whole, not burned. We ran across the yard to find our father at the table, our mother at the stove.

"Playing in the barn again before breakfast? Did you find any eggs?" She smiled playfully.

We did not understand. "But the fire!"

Her look changed. "Yes. It is very sad. It happens every day, but you get used to it. I would go through anything for the two of you, even this."

"We are so sorry," we wept. "Forgive us, forgive us."

"We do," they said, together. "We have."

Afterwards we discovered that we both had felt a tingling in our shoulders, a breath released that we had held for decades. When Father tucked us into bed that night, we fell instantly asleep.

The next morning, again we went for berries, and the house burned, and our mother died, and our father cursed us, and we wept, and we slept by the stream, and the wind rose, and the rain came, and the invisible dog barked, and a great snake went by, and we went to sleep in the barn, and we woke to find the house restored and our mother and father at the table.

This happened day after day: the berries, the burning, the death, the cursing, the weeping, the wind, the rain, the barking, the snake, the barn. We were wearied with the sadness but newly overjoyed each morning to see our mother alive again, and our father happy and full of the juice of life, rather than dried-out and bitter.

One morning after many mornings had passed, we went into the kitchen where breakfast was cooking, and our father turned from the table to speak to us, but instead of our father it was Sandor.

"Did you get your fondest wish?" he said.

"Yes," we said. "You see that we have."

"Do you want to stay?" he said.

"We will," we said. "We can't leave her to suffer this alone."

"You can, but you won't. You could, but you wouldn't," said Sandor. "You could follow me right now." He stood up, walked straight out of the house and down to the road, past the privet hedge, and out into the day's heat.

That day, again, the house burned, and we lay down first by the creek and then in the barn.

We awoke on a dark stage to an empty hall. That was the third time we died.

We walked home, and the newspaper was on the porch, and it seemed to be the same day that we'd departed, but earlier. It was Thursday, and so meatloaf night, which made getting supper together easy.

Needless to say, we never saw Sandor again.

We do not believe we will die again in this life.

IV

UDC

Dear Sister,

Well, I have quit. I know you think it is high time, but the UDC has meant a lot to me over the years, not to mention being a connection to Mother and Granddear, and a way of preserving our Southern Heritage. If you had not moved to California you would understand better. When you attend a memorial at the statue on a courthouse square, or stand at the grave of your ancestor, or see and touch the flag he fought under and died for, you are reminded that the sacrifices of so many should not be forgotten or diminished by time and changing opinions.

I hope that you and Phillip are well and that his ankle has healed up from the skiing accident. I had a nice thank-you note from Anne, who seems to be enjoying college. I did not know that Hotel and Restaurant Management had become a major, but I am sure she will do well at it. Does Will want anything special for graduation? Unless I hear otherwise I will send him a check and a Cross pen from Starmer's, as I think that always suits as a graduation present.

Bev Henderson asked me to send you her greetings the next time we wrote or spoke. I saw her at church and she is not much better but still gets out and did her Christmas baskets for the poor this year as she has done every year. I don't know that the poor really want crocheted hot pads and homemade pralines, but that is what they get, and I suppose beggars can't be choosers.

Sue Wiggins may just possibly be in touch with you about some family documentation. As secretary of the UDC she has taken it upon herself to check through all the chapter files and applications, no matter how far back, and she has had the effrontery to suggest that our ancestor C. William Harchester was not in fact an enlisted soldier who fought bravely in the Confederate Army but rather a storekeeper who supplied the Union forces with buckshot when they ran out of other munitions! I have told her that a certain William *Harkhester* has been confused with our ancestor before, and that all this has been cleared up, but I have been unable to find the proper papers. In the meantime, the chapter voted to "suspend" my membership, and so of course I resigned immediately.

Sue, I believe, is still smarting at the defeat I handed her last fall when she wanted to host the state convention with a theme of "All Is Forgiven" and return the Ohio regimental flag captured in the Battle of Ringgold Gap, Georgia, and held by our chapter, to the Museum of the Civil War in Columbus, Ohio. (The U.S. flag captured by our boys was returned to the 76th Ohio Infantry in 1916, but the regimental flag, considered a greater mark of valor in that some of our young men died in capturing it, was held back, which I believe only right and not at all deceitful as Sue

would have it.) I gave a rather rousing speech in which I
asked whether we were to cease calling it the War of North-
ern Aggression as well and suggested that Sue's *bona fides*
were at best somewhat flimsy, her ancestor having made
a *very* late arrival into the war and that as an office clerk
who never saw battle but was lightly wounded by a stray
bullet from a firing range and decorated out of pity.

Still, it hurts to be betrayed by those you have known
for so long. As you know, I have always spoken my mind,
and not everyone appreciates that, but I like to say that
you know where you stand with me, that I'll speak to
your face not behind your back. I suppose this is the
price one pays for being honest in a corrupt world.

In other news, my roses are doing well this year after a bad
bout with blackspot during the wet weather we had, and I
have been selected to manage the church bazaar this summer after repeatedly winning "best pie" for several years in
a row with my lemon chiffon. Being a widow in a married
world sometimes leads to a feeling of being the "fifth wheel,"
but my friends are very good about including me in their
social activities. Last week I went to a dinner party at the
Ledbetters', and of course I have my weekly bridge game.
There is talk at the garden club of a field trip weekend to
Bellingrath Gardens to see the azaleas, but I still have my
old trouble with carsickness and probably will not risk it.

I hope all is well with you and look forward to hearing
from you soon.

Yours as ever,
Alice

Lost and Found

I always look at births and weddings, never divorces or deaths. Divorces are just sad—the hopes of a lifetime of love and companionship reduced to a few lines of dry legalese—and deaths you will always hear about, one way or another. I have friends who can hardly wait until 9 A.M. (some still hold to 10 A.M.) so that they can start calling everyone they know to talk about who died, and how, and when the visitation will be, and which family member is in disgrace over not being at the bedside, or staying too long at the bedside, or not coming home from thousands of miles away, or showing off by buying an expensive plane ticket to come from thousands of miles away to attend the funeral.

After births and weddings—Sundays are the only day for wedding announcements, and I always look to see where they are going for their honeymoon, the Caribbean usually, if not Branson, Missouri—I move on to the classifieds section, where I scan the Lost and Found columns, mostly for pets, almost always dogs and cats but occasionally a ferret, snake, or rabbit—of course, I have to hope that the rabbit hasn't had the misfortune to meet with the ferret or snake.

When I find a match between a pet in the Lost column and one in the Found, I've won. They don't always match exactly, but if the neighborhood, color of fur, size, and so on mostly fit, I'll call the phone number for the lost pet and be sure they've seen the Found ad. You'd be amazed by how many people who have posted lost pet ads don't check the Founds, just sit back waiting for someone to see their ad and phone them. I tell them that I am from the Society for the Restoration of Lost Pets (which is true, even though currently I am the sole member) and that I keep track of these things. Most people sound surprised at first, a few a bit suspicious, but they all thank me, and I like to think I've helped to reunite some animals and people who otherwise might have remained unhappily apart.

A couple of months ago I picked up the free weekly town guide, *City Lights*, at the grocery store. It lists events, restaurants, and so on, but I was interested in it because it had a feature on my friend Alice Compton and her work with preserving old graveyards. The article on Alice was continued to the back of the weekly, and when I finished it I found myself looking idly at what turned out to be singles ads, called "People Meeting People." I had never seen these before, and it took me a while to work out the code: S for single, D for divorced, M for married (not many of those, but a few, and all included the word "discreet" in their ads); W for white and B for black and A for Asian; M and F of course; G I took to be gay, and B took me a while but then I figured out from the context was bisexual. Most of the writers could have used a copyeditor, but in general they were able to make it clear whether they were looking for a fling or a long-term partner, someone of the same age or older or younger, and so on. Dancing, taking walks, and watching movies were the most popular favorite activities.

I couldn't help myself. I started matching them up. "DWM, 43, looking for Friday-night dates and perhaps more, enjoys the outdoors, family, cookouts. No game-players, #1032" seemed a natural match for "DWF, 39, looking for nice man to date who doesn't mind children, enjoys nature, camping, laughing together, #1456." Television that night was a bore, so I got out my scissors and cut out the pairs I found, then taped them together onto a piece of paper. I found five matches that first time.

"Whatever are you doing?" said my sister, Claire Elizabeth, when she came into the kitchen and found me at the kitchen table with what must have looked like an odd craft project.

"See," I said, "they match! Imagine if you could just let them know, in case they haven't noticed, or placed the ad and then gave up."

"Yes," said Claire Elizabeth, "but you can't, can you? Surely they don't put their own telephone numbers in those ads."

"No," I said, disappointed. "I hadn't thought of that."

"Let's play Scrabble," she said, so I put away my matchmaking kit and we set up the game on the table and made some microwave popcorn to munch while we played. I think that microwave popcorn is one of the great inventions of the twentieth century. It used to be such trouble, first in the skillet, then with those odd JiffyPop things you did on the top of the stove, then popcorn poppers that became greasy and disgusting after only a few uses. Air poppers are clean but the popcorn tastes like Styrofoam. As long as you don't get greedy for every last kernel to pop and leave the bag in too long, microwave popcorn is just about perfect. Claire Elizabeth won, 305 to my 280 (she used all her letters on one play and got the extra 50 points), but I made some wonderful words, killdeer and wizard and xylem, so I was happy.

The next day, I was still curious about the singles ads. I looked at the directions for signing up. For only $10 a month, you could place one ad per each weekly issue for a month, or multiple ads each week for $15, $20, or $25 a month, I suppose to increase your chances; you were given an identification number, which others could use in responding to you, via the central office. All I wanted to do was place an ad suggesting that #1032 might be interested in #1456, and so on, and when I called the *City Lights* office and explained myself, the young woman who I spoke to said she guessed that would be OK, that there was no rule against it, as long as you paid your $10 and got a number.

I didn't initially tell Claire Elizabeth what I was doing, just made up my ad to say "A friend, SWF 1221, suggests that 1032 meet 1456, 1721 meet 1328, 1987 meet 1265, 1665 meet 1342, and 1553 meet 1873."

The next week, when *City Lights* came out, I picked it up at the store and took it home.

I called Claire Elizabeth over to the table. "Take a look at this one!" I said, pointing to mine. She read, narrowed her brow, glanced at me, glanced back at the ad. Her eyes were amused but she also looked slightly irked.

"Josephine Fern," she said, "You have gone to meddling."

"Oh, it's harmless," I protested. "A bit of anonymous matchmaking, is all."

"I guess there's no trouble in it," she said. "But still."

I pored over the ads and did it again the next week, and the next. Nothing happened, but I enjoyed thinking that people might have decided to get in touch, that they might be beginning romances I might later read about in the paper in the weddings section, and that I might possibly even recognize them by age or other characteristics.

About the fourth week, I noticed a funny thing. I was reading through ads, matching this one with that one, when I found a number, 1379, that I thought I'd already seen. And then I found it again. In one he was a DWM who enjoyed contra dancing and long walks, in another a SAM who was looking for "good times with a sexy lady of any race," in a third a WWM with an interest in bonsai, tai chi, and hopes for someone to spend time with. In each, he stated his age as 42. I called the office.

"I was just wondering," I said, "if there was a mistake with #1379, as that seems to be a listing for several different people, but they have the same identification number."

"Ma'am, we don't screen these. People can place as many ads as they pay for."

I posted my next ad with the usual matches, plus "be careful of #1379, perhaps not what he seems."

The next week, he was there again, in several guises. Who would do that, I wondered, and for what purposes? It seemed vaguely sinister. I placed another ad, this one more strongly worded: "Who is #1379 and why is he lying?" My heart beat faster as I turned these in at the weekly's office. But I felt protective of the SWFs and DWFs who might respond to him.

Then two nights ago I woke in the dark with a start. The curtains at the open window moved slowly out, then in, like breathing. Then came a slowly emerging consciousness of a presence in the room. Once, I had dreamed a ghost at the end of the bed, a young man in uniform who looked sad, but this was different. My animal self registered body warmth, breathing, a gaze directed at me. I could not see his eyes, but I could feel them on me as surely as the gazelle feels the eyes of the lion barely concealed in high grass.

Something about my own breathing must have changed.

"You should lock your doors," a voice said, a little high-pitched but male. "Don't worry, I ain't studyin' you. That's not how I get my kicks. But you need to stop spoiling my fun with your little ads, you understand?"

I didn't speak. I don't know if I could have. When I was a child I had dreams of terrible things happening, and I would scream and scream but no sound would come out. I'd wake drenched in sweat, my mouth open and my jaw tight.

As I lay there I felt the air move, and after a few seconds I heard the slight click of the front door closing. I sat up in the bed, shaking, then went to the kitchen for a glass of water.

Walking back to my bedroom I saw that Claire Elizabeth had pulled on her robe over her pajamas and was standing in the hallway.

"What are you doing up?" I said, trying to make my voice sound normal. But I couldn't hide my distress from her. I never have been able to.

"What is it, Jo?" she said, with that hawk-eyed look she gets whenever she senses trouble.

"A man," I said. "Someone was here. In the house. In my bedroom." And I told her what had happened.

What I love most about my sister is that she always takes me seriously, never scoffs or mocks. When she uses my full name, however, as our mother used to when something serious was happening—trouble *or* danger—I feel it.

"Josephine Fern Matcham," she said. "This is serious business. I'm worried for you. You may have put yourself in danger. I think you should stop."

"But this man!" I replied, my fear turning to anger as quickly as a bird takes wing. "*He* should be stopped! He's a menace. I'll call the paper, tell them their confidentiality is compromised. How did he find out who I was, where I live?"

"Fine," she said. "Make your complaint, call the police if you like, but then stop."

It suddenly, belatedly, occurred to me that my actions had endangered Claire Elizabeth as well but that she had been too good to say so, and I burst into tears.

"I am a foolish, foolish old woman!" I said fiercely, seeing myself as though from the outside and finding my recent behavior worthy of ridicule.

Claire Elizabeth just did what she always does when I cry: she led me to my favorite chair in the living room, patted me on the shoulder, went into the kitchen to put the copper kettle on to boil so she could make a pot of Earl Grey, and went and found Douglas Fur, our cat, and put him on my lap. We have had a number of cats since she moved in with me after being widowed in her fifties, but though the cats change, her habit does not. She puts the cat on my knees and goes off to make the tea.

My bad moment passed. I have given up involving myself in the singles columns, although I am still going to keep up with my animals. I called the *City Lights* offices and discontinued my account. The young woman told me that "People Meeting People" would probably be cancelled soon anyway, as the Internet was taking over the market.

I still think about the man, whose voice I heard only once but will remember always. He hasn't come back, his warning having served its purpose. But I have been having one of my recurrent dreams more frequently in the last few weeks. In the dream, I am in a familiar house, not quite one of the houses I have lived in but similar in some ways to each, when I remember that a door in the back bedroom leads to a whole other section of the house that I keep forgetting to open up and use. I go into the rooms and remember that they are haunted. They are dark and musty-smelling, and I know I can never make them sunny and fresh, no matter how hard I work, and that that is why I don't use them. I close up and lock the door, and the dream ends.

I've pondered that dream before—Mother once told me that the house is a metaphor for the self—but, since the man was here, it is as though the door won't fully close, is always just barely cracked open, so I can never completely forget about the dark rooms where something frightening exists. I cannot lull myself to sleep, as I used to, with the refrain, "Merrily, merrily, merrily, merrily, life is but a dream." It seems to me that I've played my life as though it were a game, a dream, a light dance, but now I have been tripped up and have lost my balance.

Claire Elizabeth is patient. She has seen me stumble before. Yesterday at breakfast she said she thought we were due for a trip to the mountains, Eureka Springs, perhaps.

"We'll leave Friday," she said. "Douglas can go to the kennel for the weekend. Be sure to bring your ukelele. I'll drive, and we can sing in the car on the way up. All our old favorites: 'Old Joe Clark,' 'Mr. Frog Went A-Courtin',' 'Down in the Valley.' You'll feel better, I promise."

And she's right. I will. For a time, just for a time.

But then it's all just for a time, isn't it? Temporary, but nonetheless significant.

January

JAN. 1

Well, dear journal, this is our fiftieth anniversary. Hard to believe I've kept up the habit for so many years. I know that when I began, as a young mother wishing to record the happiness I felt, the particular joys of those years, I did not expect to keep writing here for another half a century.

So, let's take stock:

House—in good shape, although I shouldn't have sprung for the new roof just last year.

Yard—dormant but well kept, raked, cleared, prepared for spring.

Papers—in order.

Heart—ticking along, though never without a pang for the loss of Charles, one year ago Christmas.

Mind—sharp as ever, as far as I can tell.

Spirit—busy, especially in dreams, and ready for the next step.

In short, everything humming along except the parts that aren't, namely the kidneys. I despise the phrase "renal failure," renal rhyming with penal and venal and bringing to mind senile, menial, and, oh, final. And the word "failure." Never let it be said that I "struggled against" and "lost my battle" to my illness. I simply got it. It simply happened. It wasn't a world war.

JAN. 2

Ran over a squirrel today. A sickening feeling. Had to run over it again to be sure it didn't suffer anymore. Having safely removed himself from the middle to the side of the road, the foolish creature dashed back out at the last minute, before I could stop. Why do squirrels do this? Throw themselves right into danger's path?

My Christmas paper-white narcissus is still blooming, although the stems are getting long and threatening to topple. I love the sweet scent but have to quarantine it in the Florida room so that the smell spreads through the house rather than overwhelming it. Sun on my back feels good this morning, beating through the windows. Will probably transplant the bulbs to the east bed later this week.

JAN. 3

A dialysis day. Tired afterwards, a bit unsteady on my legs. I stopped and bought myself a treat of cheesecake but then didn't have a taste for it by the time I got home. Next week my technician, Jeannine, goes on vacation. I'll do it then, when she won't be there to miss me. Today I brought her a small tin of fudge. She is skinny and can eat anything without gaining weight, she tells me. I will miss—or will "I"?—her bony, friendly, concerned face, her frizzy hair, and exotic earrings: feathers, beads, and, once, a pair of rattlesnake rattles.

JAN. 4

January, after Janus, the god of gates and doorways. His two faces look in opposite directions, as do I, now. Looking back, I am happy with my life and think only of its rewards, its happinesses: Charles, Thomas, and Abigail; my years of teaching; long, lazy summers at the cabin. The other parts either resolved themselves or never will. Looking forward, I see only decline, and that alone, for the most part. I've arranged for the cats, of course, but with dear Nell gone my last old friend has joined the rest, wherever they are.

I wonder whether it is right to leave this beautiful world, its light, its stars, its greens, its blues. Whether there aren't yet more friendships to be formed, evenings of laughter, moments of perfect silence. But a hospital room, a nursing home, these are not places of beauty. I want to have the last glass of champagne, toast the sunset, and choose.

JAN. 5

So, it is to be tomorrow. I have my plan, and I think I will not suffer. It is supposed to work. I must exercise mental discipline and not think too much about the doing of it. I mailed the letters today, and it would cause much unnecessary fuss if I changed my mind now. Plus I am nearly out of milk, butter, bread—just enough for tomorrow. I am trying not to be melodramatic about this. Yes, I do feel some fear, but not at the idea of going this way, just of death in general, the unknown. This will be my end, a little sooner than letting things take their course would be. And I think it belongs to me, although I can't make a good argument for it. I came into the world out of my parents' choosing, and the person they raised me to be is this person, the one who can clean a fish, pluck a splinter, pull a dog's rotten tooth, kill a spider, hold the hand of a dying man and not look away.

I have not made arrangements for you, journal, though I imagine my children may read you someday. They'll register my confusion at times, my uncertainties, but I don't think they'll find anything here that will hurt them. So, no burning.

I have had a good life, A GOOD LIFE. Seventy-five years ago I stepped through a doorway into it, and now I shall step through the doorway again. I pray only for a safe and painless passage.

[Note: *Found among the deceased's personal effects. Determine whether accompanying photo of deceased with author Eudora Welty is of monetary value. If not, shred all. Family asks to be notified only re discovery of monetary instruments.*]

Why I Live at the Albert Pike Hotel

It has nothing to do with the P.O. or family disputes or Eudora Welty, although I did know Eudora in her WPA photography days, and I don't think she'd mind my bit of playfulness. I was working as the East Arkansas stringer for the *Arkansas Gazette* in those days, the only *real* Arkansas newspaper as far as I'm concerned, first paper founded west of the Mississippi, best in the west, too. She was taking pictures of people in shacks and I was covering a local election between two men whose fairly recent ancestors had called themselves owners of the fairly recent ancestors of the people in the shacks. We drank moonshine together at a black honky-tonk and told each other our maiden-lady secrets.

All that was before I married a Rotarian and became respectable. Two children. Methodist Church. Sunday dinners. Volunteer work. Pearls. Gloves. Proper, mostly, in bed. Mrs. Harmony Carmichael, Lady. Everyone asks about his name, Harmony. Even he didn't know the real reason. Of course there was a story, there's always a story: that his mother, being the church organist, named him for her favorite musical term. In which case, good thing it wasn't Adagio or Forte. But once when his mother had had a glass of sherry at one of my luncheons, when she was up in Little Rock visiting, she told me that she had named him Harmony because he was her first boy after five girls and she had hoped that his birth would finally bring peace to her marriage, and to her marriage bed. By the time he was born, she was plumb wore out with trying, and her socks had lost their elastic after all those babies, if you know what I mean.

So Harmony it was, and Harmony he was. His life was dedicated to it. His courtroom was known for its quietness, and the reporters used to say you had to put your ear to the door to tell whether court was in session. Not only was there to be no yelling, not even a raised voice, and no untoward comments from either side, he frequently talked the litigants into settling their cases within the first hour of trial. "In a *compro-mise*," he used to say, "we promise, together, and each gets some of what he wants. A beautiful word. Com-pro-mise." Sometimes he would make the litigants repeat the word after him, if they were being particularly obstreperous.

I fell in love with him because despite his calm manner he was a powerful, I would even say passionate, man, and the contrast between his outer cool and his inner steam was too much to resist.

The only thing he insisted on was clean sheets every night. I kept the laundry busy washing and ironing and my maid busy changing them. Said he wouldn't wear garments he'd worn the day before, why should he sleep in sheets he'd already slept in? Didn't seem the same to me, but it was a small thing and I always had them changed by 10 A.M. And now that I live in the Albert Pike, I do enjoy fresh sheets every day, with no trouble to me. Guess I got used to it.

The Albert Pike. I came to live here ten years ago, when Harmony died. Put the house on the market, sold it lock, stock, and barrel, and moved my clothes and personal items into a seventh-floor suite in the Albert Pike. It suits me. I can lunch at the City Club when I want to, shop at the downtown department stores, have coffee in the morning and a cocktail in the evening, and I never have to clean house or even do my own laundry, except of course my unmentionables.

Buck, my son, though—acted like I was selling off the homeplace when I said I was getting rid of the house. "Where will we come for Christmas? What about the grandkids? How can you leave the house I grew up in? Where you and Papa were so happy?"

I said he was welcome to buy it if he wanted to, and that he and Becky, his sister, were welcome to take whatever furniture or china they wanted—better to go ahead and divide it up *before* I die and save all that nasty post-funeral squabbling (or pre-funeral skullduggery: I have known families where one or more members actually snuck into the house and *took* things while the rest of the family was at the viewing).

I did not tell him this, nor Becky, but I never liked that house. Harmony had bought it for me as a wedding present, so pleased with himself he could have burst, and I loved it because he loved it, but when he was gone I was done. It was a fine new bungalow then, with hardwood floors and big windows and a lot of open space from living room to dining room to kitchen, but it always felt sort of cramped to me, no place to go for privacy, and the houses on each side were in spitting distance of one another. You had to keep your curtains closed to dress or else you'd find yourself putting on a peep show. It did get better once the shrubbery grew up a bit, but I'd rather live out in the woods, like I grew up in, or an apartment. So the Albert Pike suits me fine.

But now the Albert Pike is to be sold. To Baptists, no less. Buck says since it's going to be a retirement home I should just stay put. But I can imagine it now: mandatory group sings, cheerful helpers, bad food. I *love* the Albert Pike: the polite, reserved staff, the Sunday dinners, the quiet, carpeted hallways, and I do not need to go into any rest home. I am only seventy and in full command of my faculties and my bladder.

Buck and Becky (yes, awfully, they were Bucky and Becky as children;

he loved Buck Rogers, and the nickname stuck) put their heads together and offered to take me for six months each, which was decent of them to make the offer but I know they would've had two cows if I'd said yes, and besides I am not a piece of baggage to be moved hither and yon, at semiannual intervals.

No, I have to find a new home. And if I can just get over the upsetness of having my very pleasant life uprooted, I am certain I will find something suitable. I could buy an apartment—I have the money—but I have sure gotten used to this hotel life. There's not really anywhere else in Little Rock I could move to, though, and downtown is going down since they built the mall. A certain *element* has crept in, and it is not conducive to the safety of widows.

So I am considering the Arlington, in Hot Springs. It is a large, comfortable, elegant place, historic without being rundown, and only an hour from Little Rock and the children. Perhaps just the right distance, come to think of it. I have managed to minimize my volunteer duties by hotel living, but Buck's wife, Cynthia, thinks nothing of dropping the girls off for the afternoon when she needs to have her hair done or go shopping, and though they are nice enough children, I just am not equipped to entertain them for more than an hour or two.

I had Buck drive me over to the Arlington last weekend, to talk to the manager. A suite is available, at a comparable rate, and I could have half-board for a modest sum. I never eat breakfast anyway, just coffee. It's the only way I've kept my figure after all these years. Becky has just blown up, after the children, but I can still wear suits I bought thirty years ago.

Another thing I like about Hot Springs is that I can pick up with my clubs, which have chapters there as well: the PEO of course, the Arkansas Federation of Women's Clubs—we call it the AFWC—and no doubt I can find a contract bridge set as well.

Buck and I had a nice drive over, talking about his job, the children, and so on. We stopped and bought peanut brittle for him to take home—I never touch it—and took a stroll along Bathhouse Row after visiting the Arlington. Even drank some fresh springwater, coming right out from underground.

"I could live to be a hundred drinking this water, if what they say is true!" I commented to Buck.

He half-smiled, in that way that makes him look just like he did as a boy when he thought he was being patient with his silly mother.

"If you do that, there'll be nothing left for us," he said, kind of laughing.

"Left for you?" I said, a little pricking-up feeling beginning on the back of my neck.

"Well," he said, looking off to one side at some crape myrtles that were just beginning to fade. "Our inheritance. What Papa left."

"Buck," I said, "You know that your Papa left what he had to me, and that I am leaving what I have equally to you and Becky."

"But what if you use it up?" he said, finally getting to the nub.

"What if I do? Are you saying you would rather have me die, or live in the poorhouse, just so you and your sister can inherit more money from me?" I was mad, and mad on top of it that Buck was spoiling this trip to Hot Springs, which had worried me more than anyone knew.

Buck winced. He could see he had gone too far. "No, Mama, of course not," he wheedled. "It's just, Cynthia'd like to move to a bigger house, and there'll be college for the girls, and before that cotillion and dresses and so forth, and it seems we have it coming to us, I'm sure that's what Papa meant, for you to stay in the house and live a modest life and then leave the rest to us, instead of spending it all on hotel living."

Well, I never!

I said, "You may drive me home now, and we will speak no more of it."

We did, and it was an icy drive in August. Buck started to speak several times but never did, my demeanor being as hard as I could make it, and I could tell he was thinking that the thing to do was just let me cool down and then I would see reason. One thing I hate is when I feel I am being managed, and that is just what he was doing—managing me. He had got over the hard part and was relieved, I could tell, despite the discomfort of it.

When I move to the Arlington, as I have really just about made up my mind to do, I will drive my own car, even though I had thought to sell it before leaving Little Rock. The porters at each hotel will help me with my cases, and I will tip them for their services. God forbid I ask anything of my son again. Ingratitude, thy name is Bucky.

Now that I am reconciled to leaving the Albert Pike, and Little Rock along with it, I am thoroughly pleased to be moving to the Arlington. Hotel life suits me. It is decorous. It is quiet. And at any time of day, you may put out the little sign that says, "Privacy, please."

Trompe L'Oeil

I

1970: Elizabeth/Ilsa

I'm sure the young couple renovating my old house thought I was a crazy old lady the day I showed up and told them my life story. The thing was, I'd just seen my own grave, and I was a bit off-balance.

I'd forgotten how hot the South could be. It was June, this past summer, and I was near fainting in my wool Chanel suit. I'd meant just to peek at the house and keep going, but I knew I needed to sit down, preferably with something cool to drink.

And so I stood in the open doorway of the house and gave a slight cough and they looked up from where they were working to strip old paint off the banisters I used to slide down as a child and hope not to get caught doing so.

They had apparently just begun to peel the layers of wallpaper from the wall by the stairs, and that's what got me started on my story.

"This is the old Billingslea place, isn't it?" I asked.

"Yeeees," the young woman said slowly, seeming to scour her brain for whatever history of the place she knew.

"Yes," I said. "I knew it. I was a girl here." I held out my white-gloved hand to her work-gloved one. "Ilsa Benn. I was Elizabeth, the eldest Billingslea girl."

After we all shook hands and introduced ourselves, they asked me into the parlor.

"Would you mind if I sat down?" I asked. "This heat . . ."

The woman, Ann, sat me in one of the chairs, brought me fresh iced tea with mint from the garden, and turned the oscillating fan toward the living room, furnished with only a couch and two chairs. They apologized for their lack of furnishings but told me that they had decided early on that they were willing to live with less and would buy only good pieces when they could afford them. I approved.

They looked at me worriedly. I must have been very pale.

"Are you all right?" she said. "We're just settling in. I'm sorry it's not more comfortable."

"Well," I said. "It's not just the heat. You see, I've just seen my own grave."

They both smiled politely, but I could practically hear them thinking.

"You must think I've escaped from the asylum," I said. "I did escape, but not from the loony-bin. My headstone states that I, Elizabeth Annabelle Billingslea, died at age seventeen of a fever. I never knew they'd actually declared me dead."

I went on to tell them that I had been sent away from the life laid out for me and learned to venture into the world itself, and that my story and the story of the house were intertwined. With that introduction, I asked, "Would you like to hear it?"

They said yes, sat down on the couch, and I launched forward. The question was really just for politeness' sake. I needed to tell the story, there, in that house, whether they needed to hear it or not. I write it down now, while it is fresh in my mind again, perhaps for that memoir I've meant to, but never found time to, write.

"This was the parlor," I began. "This was where I was sitting when Father told me I was to leave and never return. Words I had never imagined hearing."

In 1895, I was seventeen years old. The house had been in a flurry of cleaning and sewing for weeks. I was to make my debut into society in May, and my mother and younger sisters Frances and Madeleine, called Franny and Maddie, were thrilled with the prospect of parties, dances, dinners, and fancy dresses. Mrs. Townsley, the seamstress, came almost every day for fittings. I used to love to watch the dresses take shape, from choosing the cloth to the final hemming and the little tucks in the seams for a perfect fit.

My friends Virginia Sloan and Caroline Bennett were coming out as well. It was a moment in our lives that was much anticipated, on long summer nights sitting on the porch swing, as we walked to and from school in the fall, as we opened Christmas presents with hair bows and soft leather shoes and white gloves.

Its meaning to the world, the adult world, was that we were now marriageable young women, ready to put up our hair and join society in the business of being wives, mothers, and helpful volunteers in the community. I have since learned of customs in rural Greece, still current at the time of my upcoming debut, that demanded very particular items and colors of clothing for girls, young women, wives, then mothers, then widows—all of the green, the blue, the black, the belts, the necklaces, the headwear designed to reflect the stages of a woman's life in relation to men—as daughter, potential mate, wife, mother, widow—as though those things were all that defined her, as though she were no more than the sum of her reproductive and caretaking abilities.

But we were innocent then. We imagined not husbands but beaux, not the marriage bed but the excitement of a first kiss, a dance, a Sunday afternoon visit in the parlor, an ice-cream social. Girls of that class, in that time, learned of sex and childbirth from their mothers on the day of their marriage, if they were lucky, and it was largely a mystery to most of us how we had come into the world.

The parlor was always kept in readiness for guests—carpet swept, mantel and tables dusted, upholstery fresh and plumped, chandelier sparkling. It always smelled slightly lemony, from the polish used to bring out the shine in the floor and the rich wood furniture, and faintly of wax from the beeswax candles on the mahogany sideboard. Mother had a cook and a maid, both Negro women, the granddaughter and grandniece of her mammy during the days of slavery. We thought nothing of it then, thought they should and must be grateful to have work with us, in a good household.

The rest of the house was comfortably but not ostentatiously furnished. Franny and Maddie shared a room and I, as eldest, had my own. In those days I kept a diary, which I hid under my handkerchiefs, but I had caught both my sisters peeking into it and had barred them from my room unless I was present. I wrote silly things, mostly—little poems, dreams of the future, occasionally a special entry about a picnic or a party or a visit to my maternal grandmother's house in Pine Bluff.

In addition to everything else that was going on around the house, we had a painter as well. Not the common type of house painter but a painter of murals and frescoes. In those days, itinerant painters traveled the country, working on a house for weeks at a time and staying with the family, with room and board as part of his payment, while he painted.

Ours was called Monsieur LeFranc. He presented his credentials to my parents as having studied painting in Paris and London and of working for many of the finest families of the South. He specialized in *trompe l'oeil* painting—"fool the eye"—and did faux marbleizing on pillars, wood grains on banisters, complicated moulding designs for walls and ceilings, as well as frescoes, murals, portraits, and patterned stenciling.

We three girls giggled privately at his accent and his moustache, but Mother had brought us up properly and we never laughed when he was present. He did dress well, even when working, and he smelled of an exotic scent, patchouli, which none of our fathers did. Franny and Maddie were fifteen and thirteen, too young to really talk to, but I wondered sometimes what it might be like to kiss a man with a moustache. All the boys I knew were barely shaving.

Some afternoons in that early spring, my friends Virginia and Caroline and I would sit in the gazebo in our big back yard with our embroidery and talk about how many children we wanted to have, how many boys and how many girls, and what we'd name them. The gazebo was draped thickly in wisteria vines, Virginia creeper, and honeysuckle, so it was always green and shady, private and fragrant. We all imagined husbands much like our fathers, kindly and just and somewhat distant, but we did not imagine what it would be like to be wives to such men as they.

On the afternoon of one of the parties, Mother, Franny, and Maddie left me alone at home while they went to visit some out-of-town friends who were staying with their relatives down the street. The day had turned out warm, the air was close, and I had one of the "sick headaches" I'd started getting in the past year.

I lay on my bed for a little while after they left but felt I could hardly breathe in that upstairs room, so I walked down the stairs and out to the gazebo, where I thought it would be cooler.

To my surprise, Monsieur LeFranc was there, smoking a small cigar. He rose as I entered.

"Mademoiselle," he said and bowed slightly, then made as if to go.

I told him, no, he could stay, though what possessed me I don't know. I wasn't allowed to be alone with a boy, much less a man. But I wasn't sure whether he fell into the category of houseguest or servant. In my quick calculus of the moment, it seemed rude to displace him.

I sat down across from him with my book. He continued to smoke and to study me, smiling slightly when I looked up from reading. I became more and more self-conscious, and though my headache was gone I could feel that my cheeks were flushed.

"If I may . . ." he said, rising and coming to sit next to me. He looked at the book, taking it from me and touching my hand as he did so.

"The marbling on these endpapers is very fine." He traced its patterns with his fingers. "The blue, the yellow, the cream . . ."

It was just like a scene in the book Virginia had taken surreptitiously from her mother's room and read to us, but I was in it. Monsieur LeFranc's physical warmth radiated toward me. It occurred to me, as though in a dream, that our legs were touching. He took my hand and began to trace the colors with my fingers, blue yellow cream, blue yellow cream. And I lost my reason and let Monsieur LeFranc seduce me, to the scent of honeysuckle and the soft whoo-whoo, whoo of the mourning doves.

When Mother and the girls came home, I was in bed, resting again, my mind amazed at what my body had done. Monsieur LeFranc had of course asked me not to speak of this to anyone, and I didn't know if I would even tell Caroline and Virginia, but I had to tell *someone*, so after the party that night I wrote it all down in my diary.

The next day I went searching for my wide pink satin ribbon to wear around my waist. It wasn't in my room, in the drawer I kept my ribbons in, or anywhere else. I went to Franny and Maddie's room, and finally found it, crumpled, beneath Maddie's bed.

I stormed downstairs, ribbon in hand, to find her. She was sitting at the kitchen table watching our cook, Annie, make a pie.

"Maddie!" I almost shouted. "Look what you've done with my best pink ribbon! Can't you take care of anything?"

Maddie looked at me guiltily. "I'm so sorry, Lisbeth," she said. "You know I'm terrible with clothes. Not like you."

"Sorry isn't enough this time," I said, angrier than I should have been. "You have to learn. Stay home tonight from the ice-cream social to prove you're truly sorry."

"But Lisbeth—"

"Are you truly sorry or not?"

She gave in and said she'd stay home, if I said so.

I was aware of Annie watching, quietly judging me for my temper with my baby sister. But she continued to peel and slice apples, mixing them with butter and sugar and cinnamon, and so I turned on my heel and left the room.

The next day when I woke the house seemed oddly quiet. The usual morning sounds of voices, clinks of dishes and pans in the kitchen, work in the yard, all missing. The sun was well up, and no one had awakened me for breakfast. I remembered it feeling that way only once before, when my grandmother had died, and I felt a throb of fear go through me. Who could it be?

I dressed and went downstairs. It was eerily quiet. Walking past the parlor I saw Father.

"Come in and sit down, Elizabeth Annabelle." It was a command.

I sat.

He held up my diary. It looked small and defenseless in his hands.

"Is this diary yours?" he said calmly, in his best courtroom manner.

"Yes, Father," I said.

"Has anyone but you written in this diary?"

"No, Father."

"Then have you, perhaps, been making up wicked stories to amuse yourself?"

It was a lifeline. If I would just lie and say I'd made it up, I might still escape his censure. But something stubborn in me resisted. I did hope the punishment would not be too bad. There were more parties coming up that weekend.

"No, Father," I said, watching him for his reaction.

His face closed down, as though the curtains of a lit house had been drawn against me. "Then you are no daughter of mine. Pack your trunk. You will leave on the train tonight. Speak to no one. I will not have our family further disgraced." He got up and walked slowly from the room, his back straight as a ruler.

I sat where I was, in shock. Like a mechanical doll I rose, walked up the stairs, packed some clothes, a hairbrush, a framed photograph of me with my sisters. I couldn't believe it was happening, couldn't imagine how it had happened. How long would I have to stay away? What about my debut?

I sat down on my bed with the door closed and waited. At lunchtime, Annie brought me some soup on a tray. Her eyes were sorrowful, but she didn't speak. She knew about rules and what happened if you broke them.

I was lying on my bed, crying almost unconsciously, the tears rolling out of my eyes and down into my hair and ears, when the door creaked and Maddie came in. Her eyes were red, her face puffy.

"I didn't know," she said. "I didn't know! I'm so so sorry, Lisbeth." And she told me what had happened.

Angry at me for scolding her about the ribbon, she'd gone to my room to take something to "punish" me for the scolding. Looking at my hand-kerchiefs, she'd discovered the diary and read the entry on Monsieur LeFranc, not understanding its full meaning. Worried that he had done something to me that I was afraid to tell about, she had asked our mother what "seduce" meant, not intending to tell on me, only to understand. Of course Mother was horrified at her asking about such a word and before long had wriggled the whole thing out of her and read my diary. She could have kept it to herself, but she told Father.

"I'm not supposed to see you," she said. "Mother says you're leaving to go stay with Aunt Bess in New York, but they're going to tell everyone you've been stricken with fever and taken to the country to get better. Monsieur LeFranc was gone this morning. Lisbeth, please forgive me."

Of course I did, sorry that I had ever been so petty with her. After she left, I sat staring at the wall, hardly knowing that the day had passed. When Mother came for me after dark, there was no sympathy in her eyes. Annie's husband took us to the train station, and Mother hustled me into a compartment and closed the curtains before we saw anyone we knew. She sat across from me as though she were a stranger and only spoke to me once the train started up with a heave, as though it were re-luctant to move.

She told me that I had disgraced my family. That I was not worthy of it. That despite all my privileges, all my raising, I had rejected the very principles that made me a lady. She said that I would go to New York and stay with my Aunt Bess, who had very generously agreed to allow me to stay with her until I could find employment. She made it very clear that

I was not to return, nor attempt to communicate with the family. She would leave the train at Memphis, she said, and handed me my ticket.

My throat felt thick. Who was this person? Where was my loving, kind mother? I sobbed. "But Mother—"

"It's too late for that now," she said, and as I looked, finally, into her eyes, I saw that she too had been weeping. She lowered her eyes. "Your father has decided. You are lost to us now, and that is all there is to say."

Aunt Bess, my namesake, treated me decently if coolly. I found work as a seamstress—Mother had taught all three of us to sew a beautiful, tiny stitch—and slowly rose in my profession, sewing costumes for Broadway plays and then becoming a designer: the Ilsa Benn line of swimwear.

I never went back home until that day this past June. Eventually I took a subscription to the *Arkansas Gazette* and followed the wedding announcements, the birth announcements, the obituaries. Even after Mother and Father died, I left my sisters alone. I thought that surely they would find me, if they wanted to. All my family is gone now—Maddie died last year—and I needed to see the house one last time.

When I finished my story, I looked up for the first time. The fan droned. Late afternoon light slanted through the bare windows.

"Ilsa Benn," Ann said. "Of course. 'Swimwear designer to the stars.'"

I was pleased that she had heard of me, and I thanked them for listening, although I felt a bit like the Ancient Mariner. I then played my "trompe" card: "Here's how the story ends: you must be careful in removing that old wallpaper, perhaps even call in a conservator. Beneath it are extraordinary *trompe l'oeil* paintings, courtesy of Monsieur LeFranc."

They promised they would.

I stood. I'd kept them long enough, and said so. My hotel was just down the street, and even though the man, Davis, was forceful in his insistence, I wouldn't let them call a taxi. At the doorway, I paused. I wanted to leave some kind of benediction, after my sad tale. "I return to New York in the morning, and I don't think I'll be back again. I hope you'll be happy here. This house *has* known happiness and I think it will welcome it again."

II

2010: Ann

After forty years of living in this old Victorian, I am loathe to part with it. But I think I'm almost ready. I'll know for certain if I pick up the phone to call the realtor and my hands comply in dialing her number. If they're still reluctant, I'll wait. It is my hands that know this old house best and have the most to lose in letting go.

I used to hear people say "it's just too much house for me now," and I was secretly scornful. I love inhabiting the many spaces of a house— breakfast room, kitchen, living room, bedroom, study, sewing room, back porch, bathroom with its clawfoot tub, plus the expansive back yard with our big kitchen garden. But since my husband, Davis, died two years ago, I feel that I'm knocking around in all these rooms. I find myself wanting a beautiful, petite shell that I can curve into, inhabit fully, keep tidy and clean without expending too much energy on mere maintenance, as I do now. I want one beautiful rosebush, pots of pansies or pinks depending on the season, a small front porch with padded wicker chairs for visitors, and the ease of being able to lock the door and walk away for a month at a time, should the spirit move me.

We have lavished care on this house for as long as we have known it, scraping and painting and repairing and rewiring, replumbing, restoring, furnishing, preserving. Every time I drive up to it, I feel proud and happy at how we saved it from sure ruin.

Davis and I were newly married, both of us full of more energy and optimism than I have ever had before or since. He had begun his first job as a history professor at UALR after finishing his PhD in Wisconsin. We were delighted to be back in the South, devoted to the idea of homestead-ing in the once-grand areas of downtown that had seriously deteriorated. Surely smug, somewhat self-centered, we saw ourselves as new-style fron-tiersmen, making the Quapaw Quarter safe for the middle class. I forgive our young selves our hubris.

For years we lived in a work-in-progress. We moved into it with only the bedroom and the kitchen habitable and worked our way through the rest. On evenings and weekends, we worked together. Days, I divided my time between the yard and the house, switching from one to the other when I was tired. Even though the house was approaching one hundred at the time, I couldn't imagine being old myself.

But an old lady, who had lived there as a child, was the cause of the second married quarrel between me and Davis. (The first had been over the issue of women being ordained as priests in the Episcopal Church. There was much talk of it in those days, and it would happen in only a few years. The argument started when Davis said, laughingly, "Wives and mothers as priests? I don't recall any apostles named Susan or Jane or Matilda." He had, much later, changed his mind when our daughter Liz decided to enter the priesthood. Sometimes you have to wait years in a marriage to be proved right.)

We were working in the foyer on a hot Saturday in June. Davis was sanding down the staircase banister, and I was just beginning to pull down the layers of ancient wallpaper. The front door was open for the breeze, and at first neither of us noticed the tiny woman in a red Chanel suit with matching hat and shoes who stood at the threshold, waiting for us to see her.

"Hmhm," she cleared her throat. We looked up at the same time. Her chic outfit was in stark contrast to my paint-stained chinos, tennis shoes, and one of Davis's old shirts. Davis was in a ratty T-shirt and shorts, in contrast to his usual crispness.

"This is the old Billingslea place, isn't it?" she asked.

And then she told us a story from another time, a story that couldn't happen today, of being a girl in this house, eager to grow up and get married but still in many ways a child, loving pretty dresses and hair ribbons and parties. A traveling artist, a Monsieur LeFranc, as he called himself, was working in her house on the *trompe l'oeil* paintings we'd eventually uncover and preserve, when he seduced her one afternoon. The rest of the family was out, she was in the gazebo, one thing led to another—he was probably adept at this—and then her whole life fell apart when her parents found out what had happened. The painter was sent away immediately, she was put on a train to New York to live with an aunt, and she never saw her family again.

It was strange, sitting there listening to her tell her story, almost in a trance of remembering. I wondered at the telling, but at some point I understood that she could not *not* tell it, and that we were her needed audience.

When she finished, she had looked up, shaken her head, and smiled a tiny apologetic smile. She said she was so sorry to have troubled us, that she hoped we'd take good care of the house, and that she expected we'd be happy there. She insisted on walking back to her hotel, despite Davis's desperate wish to at least call a cab.

After she left we looked at each other but waited until she was suitably out of earshot, a little way down the sidewalk, before speaking.

"What an amazing story," I said.

"Yes," he said. "Amazing. Perhaps even fantastic."

Still caught in the spell of her story, I wasn't sure what he meant. "Fantastic? As in untrue?"

"How do we know she is who she says? Maybe Elizabeth Annabelle Billingslea did die at age seventeen of a fever. Maybe this woman thought there was something to be gotten here."

"Davis!" I said. "I really do not believe you. Aren't you curious about the painting? If that's true, then she's true."

We pulled a corner of the wallpaper a bit further back. Something like the edge of a fan, or a flower, appeared, a washed-out blue with rose beneath.

"So it was her," I said triumphantly. "We can call the Historical Commission on Monday and ask someone to come down and take a look."

Davis was silent, and when people are silent I tend to speak. I wish I wouldn't, but I do.

"What an incredible woman," I said. "To take a terrible situation like that, being removed from all you've ever known, and make such a life. Don't you think?"

"Hmm," said Davis. "Of course, if you think about, well—if she'd just kept her legs together, she'd never have had to leave."

It was early days for feminism in Arkansas then, and I too had been raised to safeguard my virginity, but I still couldn't believe my ears. And Davis had never said anything so coarse, or so chauvinistic, in my presence.

I told him I was appalled and asked, "What if that had been your daughter? Would you honestly have sent her away from the family forever, for one mistake?"

"Those were different times," he said, with infuriating calm, "and you live by the rules of your times." He turned back to work on the banister.

"Well then I hope we never have any daughters together," I said. "I hope we never have children, period!"

I was furious with an anger that had nowhere to go, so I threw down the open boxcutter I'd been using on the wallpaper (leaving a permanent nick in the hallway floor's heart-pine boards) and stomped upstairs, where I scrubbed the clawfoot tub to within an inch of its life.

I didn't speak to him at supper, nor for the rest of the evening. I couldn't think what I might say to this man I'd thought I knew, not until he said something first. He would look at me occasionally, appraisingly, and then go back to eating or, later, reading. All night I dreamed of trains on dark tracks, empty, abandoned stations, and rusting cars on sidings.

In the morning, Davis rose before me and went for a run. When he returned I was at our round oak table in the kitchen with my second cup of coffee.

"*Pace?*" he said. He had studied Latin in school.

"Yes, *pace*," I agreed, feeling a little sad. I had thought that being soulmates meant we would agree about everything, but I was learning that the very things I valued about Davis—his love of history, his respect for tradition—also made him less than progressive, in times that valued change.

"The gazebo. I was thinking. Let's restore it, too, instead of tearing it down as we were talking about. The wisteria vines are still there, and it would make a nice place for us to sit and have a drink or read together."

Davis's peace offerings, I was to learn, were never direct but were nevertheless heartfelt. As the father of three daughters himself, he would come to learn the particular pains and hopes of fathers, feel the conflict between protecting them and letting them grow into independent women.

I sit in the gazebo just about every evening now, saying goodbye. It is a slow goodbye, not like Ilsa's abrupt leavetaking. I smell the honeysuckle, listen to the mourning doves, catch drifts of conversation and smells of steaks cooking across my neighbors' back yards. When the fireflies come out, I go in. I turn on the lights, close the drapes, fix myself supper, and ponder the next chapter of my life.

Years ago, after the girls grew up and moved out, I would sometimes hear the sound of someone weeping, upstairs in the sewing room. I'd never see anything there, of course, and occasionally convinced myself it was our old pipes whining, or two branches squeaking as one rubbed against the other in the wind. After Davis died, I'd wake to the sound of my own tears, seeming at first to come from somewhere outside of me, until I woke fully into my own body's grief. Neither troubles me now. Perhaps those ghosts are laid to rest. I sleep well these days, better than I have in years, and my dreams are filled with interesting people with whom I have intense and lively conversations about art, music, the meaning of life, as though I were a teenager again.

III

Coda, 2011: Reverend Liz

Mother died suddenly last night. She's been clearing out the house, and I was worried she'd work herself too hard. She's always been that way, pushing just a little beyond her strength to get the next thing done. The doctor thinks her heart gave out.

I think it was peaceful, though. The mailman saw her through the window this morning—she'd died before closing the drapes—and thought something wasn't right, and called me. He's been on that route his whole career, known me since I was a child, and he knew he could find me at the church.

She was sitting in her favorite chair, a glass of white wine next to her, the reading lamp casting its halo, and she'd been reading her favorite poet, Gerard Manley Hopkins. We'll have "Pied Beauty" for her funeral. I can hear her reciting it, "Glory be to God for dappled things . . ."

So hard, seeing her there but not there.

I'll ask Jim Sloan from St. Mark's to do the service. Dad's death was expected. I officiated at his service at his request, a final confirmation of his approval. But this is too hard, too sudden. I want to sit with our family, and I want to be able to grieve her good life, and our loss, and believe that she was happy as she died, and that eventually we will be, too.